'Pretty in pink,

MW01699365

'Glad you wore something special now? You're the most beautiful woman here.'

'It doesn't feel like me,' she told him, blushing at the compliment.

His eyes roamed over every inch of her face with a look of such blatant desire that she almost gasped. But as suddenly the look was gone. 'You should try not feeling like you more often,' he suggested, his lips taunting her.

Sally Heywood was born in Yorkshire. After a spell in London she now spends part of each year writing in her cottage in a remote fishing village on the East Coast. She has written over twenty books for Mills & Boon and it is the nearby moors, together with a passion for sailing, that provide her inspiration. When she is not writing she travels extensively with her two daughters in a constant search for new locations and the perfect romantic hero.

TIDES OF PASSION

BY

SALLY HEYWOOD

MILLS & BOON PTY LIMITED
SYDNEY • AUCKLAND • MANILA
LONDON • TORONTO

This edition published under arrangement with Harlequin Enterprises BV

Published by
Mills & Boon Pty. Limited
3 Gibbes Street, Chatswood, NSW 2067 Australia

First published in Great Britain 1992
Australian copyright 1992
New Zealand copyright 1992
Philippine copyright 1992
First Australian Paperback Edition January 1993

ISBN 1 86386 311 7

Printed and bound in Australia by
Griffin Paperbacks, South Australia

CHAPTER ONE

THE rhythmic booming of the sea beneath the house accompanied Jane's thoughts all morning. As the tide receded she worked on in a silence broken only by the pure call of sea-birds until the light began to fail. Soon she would have to stop, she told herself. There was a meal to be cooked, sketches to be made. And one more evening alone with just the radio for company and the sound of the sea surging back under the house as the tide returned.

She smiled to herself, mocking the qualms she felt about living in such a remote spot, and began to put the finishing touches to her canvas, surveying the rich tapestry of colour with a critical eye. Then she stepped back, giving a satisfied yawn. That was enough for one day. Time for supper.

Pulling off the blue band that kept the soft ripple of pale blonde hair in place, she shook her head, feeling her hair fly wild and free as the tension eased, then she made her way dutifully over to the sink to clean her brushes ready for the next day.

Despite her solitude a feeling of contentment filled her. It had been a good day. She really felt she was making progress now she didn't have to worry about pleasing Ivan or trying to satisfy the rather predictable taste of his clients at the gallery.

She could stretch herself, paint as *she* wanted, and she revelled in the freedom it brought.

One thing, though, nobody at art school had ever said how tiring it was to paint all day. She smiled; an Olympic training programme should be part of the course. She would put it to her ex-tutor next time she went to see her.

Cold water swished over her slender wrists at the old-fashioned sink, taking with it all her tiredness. Throughout the summer, when everything had seemed as if it was falling apart, her luck had suddenly changed, leading her to this isolated house on the estuary.

A white-weather-boarded, put-together sort of place, standing on stilts partway out over the sands, it had become available when the holiday season was over at what was a nominal rent and, because it was fully equipped for letting, all she needed to do was walk in and set up her painting equipment in the high white space of the main room and get to work. An unexpected bonus was its other main room, a conservatory with spectacular views of the river and the distant sea. Jane was drawn to the view now as soon as she had arranged her brushes to dry.

The last light of the afternoon was caught in the fragile curving glass of the dome, scattering in splinters of silver and pale gold over the bleached wooden floor. She shook out her hair again, feeling the light cascade around her, and her steps led her automatically to the double doors and out on to the balcony that ran round three sides of the house.

With both elbows propped on the balustrade, she turned to gaze up-river. She was becoming a connoisseur of sunsets these days. The lustre of evening gold enriched the flat sheen of deep water in mid-river and gilded the humps of banked sand laid bare by the tide. They lay in voluptuous curves, like golden limbs among pools of peach satin, and her fingers itched for her paintbrush again. But she knew she had done enough for one day. With the light failing fast it would be dark before she managed to set up a new canvas.

Instead she tried to commit every nuance of colour to memory as she breathed in the tonic of clean, cold air blowing in from the sea. It tingled her senses and made her glad to be here. Glad to be alone. Glad to be facing the challenge of the months ahead with her goal like a pure light guiding her on. Nothing was going to deflect her from that path again.

After a moment or two she made her way round the side of the house to check the washing she had hung out earlier. It was dry now, and she quickly unpegged it and bundled it under one arm. Here a wind harsh as salt whipped her to the bone. It snatched at her breath and made her shiver inside her T-shirt, and she gasped with the sharpness of it, her hair lashed into blonde snarls and flying out in all directions. With a gasp she turned to go in, but just before she stepped inside her glance alighted on something far out on the mussel beds near the waterline.

It was too large to be a sea-bird and too white to be a fishing boat. It was glistening in the elongated rays of the sun.

Curious, Jane went back inside, dropping her bundle on to a chair and reaching for the brass telescope provided by the owners for the bird-watching visitors. Pulling the hard cylinder to its greatest extension, she went back on to the balcony and peered through, focusing on the shoreline.

At first all she could make out was a blur of flecked water, silver and black, and the dabbing heads of sea-birds on the sandbars.

Then she swept the shore and trapped a moving shape in the lens, but despite further manoeuvring she lost it and could only make out the solid white hull of what looked like a power-boat fetched up on the shoal.

Foam laced in dazzling points around its stern. Now she'd got it firmly in focus she could see it as clearly as if she were down there on the beach herself. She could even see the links of the anchor chain where it lay like a snake in the sand. She adjusted her position, and single red letters rose into view. B-a-r-b-a—— Jane squeezed her watering eyes for a moment, then tried again. *Barbarossa*. Some pirate, she thought humorously, to fetch up on a sandbank.

Then she lowered the telescope and gave a puzzled frown. It looked as if they'd misjudged the entrance to the creek and now they'd run aground. What idiots! But it wasn't the boat that had first drawn her attention. It had been something, or someone, moving about near the shoreline.

She lifted the telescope again and swept the wide expanse of shingle until she came to the moving shape that had first attracted her attention.

It was a man. He was threading his way between the pools and over the shingle banks. She tried to work out where he was heading, but he was still too far away to be more than a blur. Though he was in black, every atom of light seemed to stream towards him with the sea like a painted canvas behind him. He cut a dazzling figure among the dunes.

Jane gauged his progress with a frown, wondering where he was heading for with such an air of purpose. Clearly had some destination in mind. But this was the only house on the foreshore. Behind it was a waste of marram grass and shingle, then the causeway, the island with its huddle of cottages, and beyond the narrow strait, and only then, was the mainland, with its roads and lights and people.

Within the circle of the telescope's lens she could see a pair of canvas shoes held firmly in one hand, the bottom of a pair of black denims rolled to reveal tanned muscled calves. She refocused in the hope of catching a glimpse of his face. His hair was black, very thick, quite short and sharply cut, but he was turned at an angle, checking the ground in front of him, and all she saw was a severe profile and a pair of black sunglasses.

She lowered the telescope with a slight grimace. He was surely heading for the house. There was nowhere else for miles. But she didn't want visitors. Not anyone. And least of all a dark, powerful-looking stranger with an air of brooding purpose about him.

The thought of how defenceless she was sent an unaccustomed trickle of fear down her spine.

She stepped back inside the conservatory and thought wildly of shutting the door and pretending there was no one at home. Then she bit her lip. The man was obviously in difficulties. Even if the silly idiot had managed to dump his boat on the sands she couldn't just write him off. But couldn't he read a chart? Didn't he know the estuary was treacherous? Hadn't he seen the buoy?

Day-tripper, she thought disparagingly, even though he didn't look like one.

For a moment she stood in the doorway between the balcony and the conservatory, unable to go in or out, wondering what to do for the best. She felt like glass herself, liable to break at the slightest contact. Go away, she whispered. I don't want you.

A rapid glance over the balcony showed he wasn't going to go away.

She braced herself, the telescope, long and hard and cold between her fingers, like a weapon of defence. Raising it again, she could see he was nearer by the second.

She watched him climb to the summit of a high sloping shingle bank, his form silhouetted against a backdrop of harassed pewter-coloured clouds. He was broad-shouldered, with an athlete's compact power, standing for a moment as if to challenge the raging sky.

And then he began to descend, and she watched mesmerised as he turned towards her, because for an instant he looked like some marauding barbarian preparing an assault on an alien fortress, and her fingers tightened round .the long cylinder of the telescope, transfixed by the sense of primitive power in the way he sensed the air. And her fingers whitened, for it was as if he had seen her, his face, framed as clearly as in a photograph in the hard diameter of the lens, looking into hers.

She felt the breath leave her body in a drawn-out sigh. He was darkly gorgeous, his face exhibiting a mixture of aggressive power and a sort of ravaged, lived-in cynicism—as if he'd see it all and done it all and found himself unmoved by the world, yet the chiselled features, a symmetry of angled bone and jaw, and his wide, firm mouth, hinted at compassion and humour too. His eyes, still hidden behind the black glasses, would be the key.

Astonished at her own reaction, she tracked him until he came close enough to see without the aid of the telescope, then she watched him stride down the last long slope towards her sanctuary until he reached the sands below the house.

At the foot of the six slender columns holding it above the waterline he came to a stop and lifted his head. By now Jane's nerves were wound tight. She held her breath as their eyes met.

There was a pause. Then he spoke, and she heard his voice for the first time. 'Am I allowed up?' he asked.

His voice sent a shiver of surprise right through her. Smoky and rich, with an actor's strength, it was pure pleasure to listen to. And the surprise of it was he wasn't even English as she assumed, but American. More than ever she wanted to know what he was doing here.

Gripping the balustrade with both hands, she stared down at him, unable to force an immediate reply that wouldn't betray the electric impact he was having. Fingers of wind wound her hair in endless knots and looped and lifted it, and as their eyes locked time seemed to hesitate while the world changed gear.

A strange conviction stole over her—he would never again be at such a disadvantage, looking up at her, asking permission to enter her hideaway. Down there on the beach he was safe. As safe as a man like him ever would be. And at this moment she was aware of a desire to keep him there, to prevent him from breaking into the fragile structure of her life. He was a threat, and all she had to do was send him away.

Then he called up to her again, and her power crumbled, for his voice was softer, full of amusement. 'Hey! I am real. How about you?'

He held both arms wide as if to show how harmless he was, charming her at this obvious pretence, one hand still clutching the canvas shoes, a bag slung over one shoulder. There was a smile, drawing her in, confusing her mind.

Leaning forward and grasping the balustrade with both hands, Jane made a last-ditch effort to keep him where he was. 'There's nothing I can do,' she called down. 'I can't help you.'

For the space of a second a small furrow appeared on his brow and he gestured towards the thin line of surf that marked the incoming tide. 'How long have I got to reach civilisation?'

The implication that her reaction was less than civilised made her blush. 'What do you want me to do?' She glanced helplessly at the distant shape of his boat.

'Provide an engineer and a few spare parts, but, failing that, I'll settle for a phone,' he smiled up at her.

'There's a phone on the island,' she told him, the excuse coming out ready-made. 'You have to cross the causeway to it by foot.' Did he know about the tide?

He smiled. He knew about the tide. 'You're inviting me to drown myself, are you?' The black lenses glinted fractionally, but for some reason Jane felt she detected a more humorous lift to his lips.

She took it as an opportunity to ask, 'Why don't you stay with your boat and float it off when the tide comes back?'

He seemed irritated by the question, and she realised she must have misjudged the humour, for his lips weren't smiling at all. But as long as she didn't invite him up there was nothing he could do. She watched him give an impatient shrug. 'That's the obvious course. But the engine's dead. I thought it safer to anchor so I could get ashore for help. I need a phone,' he explained again.

That made sense, she told herself. 'Have you called the coastguard?' she asked.

He gave her another violent appraisal. 'Look, I'm not a total fool,' his voice grated. 'It's the first thing I did. Now what about letting me use your phone so I can put a few calls through?' He hesitated as if it was an effort to offer anything resembling a request, adding more pleasantly, 'Call your dad, will you? Let me have a word with him, there's a good girl.'

Jane bristled. 'I doubt whether he'd hear me,' she replied in offish tones. 'The last I heard he was sunning himself on one of the Costas with a new wife.'

She didn't know whether she was gratified to see him laugh aloud at this or not, but at least it took some of the heat out of their exchange.

'Look, let me up anyway. I'm quite harmless, and it's the wrong time of year for paddling in the sea.' He indicated his bare feet. 'I expect all this standing about without any shoes on will give me pneumonia.' He gave her that look again, half arrogant, half little-boy pleading, the latter, she suspected, being pure pantomime.

Knowing that he had driven her to do what he'd expected her to do from the start, she put out one hand to show he'd won.

'Come up, then,' she said.

There was a gate at the top of the beach ladder, and she fumbled with the catch. She didn't want to come face to face with him. His force of character was apparent even at a distance, and it made her feel nervous even when she was subjected to it only at long range. That turbulent look of his had the seeds of a thousand black deeds in it. But she couldn't leave a man to drown, for soon the tide would be hurtling back under the house.

When the gate opened he ascended the ladder with rapid ease, his dark head quickly on a level with the balcony and then the whole formidable bulk of him rising up, blocking out the sun, his shadow wrapping her like doom in a complete embrace. She heard the gate clang shut.

Unable to help herself, she stepped back. He was far more powerful in real life than seen diminished through the lens of a telescope. He moved forward, back to the sun, and Jane side-stepped so she could see him properly. He wore an air of violence like a cloak. The jaw she had admired for its strength through the lens was hard-boned, his physique, already approved for its fitness, was, close up, very definitely all male, compounding his aura of black will like a positive charge that made the air crackle and vibrate around him. She retreated helplessly until her back was touching the delicate glass of the conservatory.

The eyes behind the sunglasses must have swept her fragile form with as close an appraisal as her own, for he said on a note of surprise, 'I thought you were about fifteen from down there. A schoolgirl.' He seemed rather affronted that she was not.

The way the lenses tilted slightly told her his glance was still taking in every detail of her appearance, lazing over the female shape under the T-shirt, especially the fact that she wasn't wearing a bra, and over her slender waist and down the long brown length of her legs in the skimpy black shorts. Her clothes seemed suddenly moulded to her body, and she tried not to flinch as he prolonged her subjection to his appraisal, only bringing it to an end when he said, 'Obviously even I can make mistakes.' Then he lifted his head. 'Is your father really abroad?' When she nodded he demanded, 'Who's here with you, then? Your mother?'

Jane shook her head, still in a daze, still too stunned by the dark energy he seemed to emit to offer any explanation. She felt winded. There must be something the matter with her.

He frowned at her silence. 'You're surely not alone out here?'

There was a scandalised look on his face, but when she nodded he gave a shrug. 'No wonder you look alarmed! But don't worry, you can trust me. I'm eminently respectable—though I suppose I would say that, wouldn't I?' he laughed, a deep sound from the core of his being that struck her at once with its warmth, but before she could respond he gave a glance over the dunes to the abandoned power-boat. 'I suppose you're always getting folk piling on to the sands?' He swung to face her, fixing the black lenses on her, his tone of self-mockery disarming her for a moment.

'I haven't been here long enough to find out,' she admitted. 'I missed the summer.' She tried to see behind the lenses. 'What do you intend to do now? Are you just going to leave it there?'

'I'm entirely in your hands.' He was still grasping his shoes, and now he spread his arms wide and for a moment they were both laughing without any apparent reason, and Jane felt a catch in her throat which she quickly cleared with a nervous cough. He was devastating, but he wasn't for her. He was just passing through, that was all. She was obviously more lonely than she realised, and it was playing tricks with her imagination. It had been days since she'd actually spoken to anyone. God, she thought, why do I have to stand goggling at him like some dumb schoolgirl? He'd been right to ask to see her father!

Aloud she said, 'I'm afraid you'll have to wait for low water in order to cross the causeway to the island to get help. You'll be able to get back on to the mainland from there quite easily, there's a footbridge and a good road on the other side. But at least I've got a phone. If you want to ring anyone—I mean . . .' She paused. 'Maybe you'll want to tell your wife where you are?'

Her tone mocked the man behind the black lashes, and he knew it. As if needing the extra message only his eyes could express, he pulled the glasses slowly down away from his face. Jane felt her lips part. Another surprise, her senses informed her. Eyes a shade of far-seeing blue she would despair of ever capturing on canvas.

'There is,' he said, picking up on her words and holding her glance, 'no Mrs Mitchener.' Thoroughly at ease, he leaned against the balustrade. 'So now that makes us equal, doesn't it?'

'I don't know what you mean.' Jane's voice was never wispy, but now it was. She cleared her throat again. 'I suppose I ought to tell you there is a problem.' She paused, wondering how he would react to what she had to say. 'The thing is, you can't get off here until low water.' Shivers ran up and down her spine as the meaning of what she was saying hit her too. 'It's about six o'clock now,' she explained. 'It'll take till ten or so for the tide to come right back in. Then there's another six hours—I'll have to check the tide tables for you—but the causeway's only crossable half an hour each side of low water. I'm sorry,' she added as if it were her own fault, 'you're not going to be able to get away till about four in the morning.'

She expected a violent outburst, some of that leashed energy to come raging out at the frustration of being trapped here half the night, but to her astonishment he took the news with a nonchalant shrug. 'That's life,' he said. 'Lucky I came prepared for a picnic.'

He swung the canvas bag from his shoulder, and she was surprised to discover that it really did contain picnic things. A bottle of wine and some interesting-looking boxes appeared. 'Here,' he said, thrusting the whole lot into her hands. 'Can you do anything with that lot? I think you'll find some hot soup in there somewhere.'

'I wondered what people did on power-boats once they'd got to where they're going,' she said, trying not to flinch when, quite accidentally, the back of his hand brushed the inside of her wrist. 'There's an enormous amount of food for one person,' she added hurriedly, trying to play down the blush that was spreading over her cheeks. Maybe somebody had let him down, she thought wildly, though she couldn't imagine anyone capable of such folly.

He was smiling, with an expression that added an extra dimension to his words. 'I take it you're not going to throw me back to the mermaids just yet, so may I wash my hands? Please?' He was obviously putting on his best behaviour. 'Engine oil doesn't go too well with roast chicken,' he added when she didn't react.

'I'm sorry,' she caught herself apologising again, her blush turning an even deeper shade of rose. 'You'd better come inside.'

After she'd pointed out the bathroom and fetched him a clean towel she went into the kitchen with the contents of his bag and grabbed for a bottle of gin she hadn't got around to opening, checked the casserole, riddled the wood-burning stove, then tried to quench the giddy feeling that seemed to be taking her over.

Now it was dusk, the air a purple haze, with only reflections from the sea flecking the glass with stars while they both moved in the shadows cast by the potted jungle plants between the chairs. He was like a force of nature, pretending to be tamed, treading with a power that seemed second nature, taking possession of the unfamiliar room by the sheer force of his male energy.

Drink in hand, he was pacing nervously back and forth like a caged animal, a brooding expression on his face as if there was something he wanted to say but didn't know how to start. His indecision didn't last long. 'So tell me,' he began, 'how long have you been here?'

'In this house? About six weeks.' She set the drinks on a rattan table and considered where it might be safe to sit.

'And your father normally lives here, does he?' he continued.

'My father?' She sat down in an armchair as far away as she could. 'You seem very interested in my father,' she said, rather bemused. 'I can't think why. He's lived in Spain for three years. I haven't seen him since Mum's funeral. But I get the odd postcard.'

He gave a look whose meaning she couldn't fathom, but persisted with his interrogation. 'So who was here before you moved in?'

She shrugged. 'It was let to different people every week—bird-watchers, couples with children, just holiday-makers.'

'So you live alone?' he persisted.

'You've already asked me that.'

Jane felt annoyed at being given the third degree, but before she could object he said, 'I find it impossible to understand why a beautiful young woman like yourself should choose to live like a nun in a convent.' His brow was darkly lowering, as if she was holding out on him.

'I don't see what it's got to do with you!' she exclaimed. 'But if you're worried about any lurking boyfriend you needn't be, because there isn't one.' Looking at him now, she rather wished there was, for he couldn't hide the temper of impatience he was in, and she wished he would at least sit down; this constant feline prowling was stringing out her nerves like anything.

'So it's just you?' He obviously didn't believe her, and she began to feel frightened. It was madness to invite a complete stranger into the house, no matter how handsome. Yet she couldn't have left him to drown either. She drew up her knees and wondered if the brass telescope would be a suitable instrument of defence should she need one.

He seemed unaware of her sudden misgivings, because he was still prowling around, picking things up and getting them down. 'I like your taste,' he conceded as he carefully replaced a ceramic figure she'd brought back from Greece. 'You have a good eye. Are you interested in art, by any chance?'

She nodded grudgingly. 'You make it seem like a crime.'

He held her glance for what seemed like an age, but there was no way of discovering what lay behind that enigmatic mask.

'It so happens I'm a painter,' she felt forced to admit. The look of disbelief that suddenly swept across his face goaded her to add, 'I exhibit in London.' After the fiasco with Ivan in the summer it was sticking her neck out to put it like that, but his manner was beginning to make her livid. He was the idiot who'd crashed his boat, not her, yet he was treating her to this weird inquisition when it was obvious he didn't believe a word she said. She had half a mind to point him towards the studio, but then changed her mind. Why the hell should she? She had nothing to prove, and his manner was appalling.

'Are you scowling?' came his velvet voice out of the semi-darkness. 'I'm the one who should be doing that.' He came to stand over her. 'Is it asking too much to have a light on?'

Jane sighed. 'I'm surprised you haven't noticed.'

'What?'

She glanced round at the bare walls. 'No electric light. It's oil, and I try to be careful.'

As a concession she got up and went over to the lamp on the table. She felt him watching her as she lit a match and fiddled with the wick. Soon a glowing halo made the shadows deepen outside its orbit. In the pool of light she turned. 'All right?'

'Exquisite.' He was standing on the rim of shadow, half in and half out of the light, his eyes cobalt, bright and provoking, looking suddenly and intimately into hers. She felt a prickle of unbidden desire spread itself over her skin like a rosy veil. It was the desire to be touched, to feel his hands caress her body, knowing they would be as velvet and seductive as his voice. Furious with herself, she went over to the window and pretended to look out. The river was quite black now. He came to stand beside her, and she felt her nerves prickle with alarm.

'If you look carefully,' he said, after a silent moment, 'you can see the anchor lights of *Barbarossa*. See?'

He was trying to soothe her, some sensitive antenna picking up the fact that something was wrong.

She pretended to strain her eyes and peer into the darkness. She couldn't feel a flicker of interest in *Barbarossa*, for now he was standing so close that she could smell the rich, lemony scent of some masculine cologne. Neither of them spoke, but their breaths made two misty orbs on the glass in front of them.

With a sudden movement Jane jerked away. It was no good. She could tell what was going to happen next, and she mustn't allow it.

'This place was built by a famous concert pianist,' she babbled. 'It's lovely and open, isn't it? He wanted to be somewhere quiet, so he could practise without disturbing anybody. I suppose he liked the light, the effect of the clouds, the glittery patterns from the water on the glass when the sun shines . . .' Her words trailed away into silence under the blaze of his blue eyes. There was the night to get through, and already her senses were singing one song and her common sense another.

She started back as he began to prowl towards her, but when she saw his expression it was obvious there was something else on his mind. 'Will you show me your paintings?' he demanded softly. 'Where are they? In here?'

Jane felt her thoughts jerk to a halt. 'I don't show them.'

He stopped halfway towards the door. 'You said you exhibited in London.'

'Well, I did. But not any more.'

'Why not?' He was watching her intently.

'It didn't work out.' She didn't add that the gallery owner was a crook; something held the words in.

'Show me,' he commanded.

'I'd rather not.' It was a battle of wills.

But there was no contest. He simply turned with a massive shrug, picked up the oil lamp and, holding it above his head, made for the adjoining room. 'In here, are they?' Before she could protest she registered the force behind the way he flung open the door. Then there was silence and the light leaped and danced against the wall.

Jane stood in the darkness, fuming, but unable to take the necessary steps to turn him out.

He was gone long enough to have inspected every single painting, finished and unfinished, ten times over. She failed to understand what had made him so determined to see them, or why he was taking so long over it. He didn't look the type to spend time in art galleries.

The minutes stretched, and she began to feel as if she was being stripped to the skin, humiliated by a feeling of helplessness as she lived through the assault of those cobalt eyes on her secret self.

She hovered outside the door, willing him to come out, willing it to end.

Then eventually the light came back in a golden flood as the door swung open and the room was swimming in it, and it was spotlighting the thrust of his hard-boned face and his eyes were brilliant with some kind of astonishment in them. The floor creaked as he moved across towards her with the lamp held aloft as if to expose to his gaze every nuance of her expression.

'It's you,' he intoned at last. 'You're Hutton. And I thought it was some guy, some real old guy. . . painting his heart out here in the wilds.' The lamp flickered. 'But it's you,' he breathed as if it still hadn't sunk in. 'I can't believe it.'

CHAPTER TWO

JANE felt trapped in the pool of light, as if by being subjected to his examination he could extract some sort of confession from her.

She put out a hand to ward him off. His eyes were searing, searching, remorselessly analysing her every gesture. Without uttering a word he managed to express a black violence, an unfocused aura of wanting that bewildered her.

'What is it?' she whispered. 'What have I done?' Was he going to humiliate her for confessing she was a painter, ridiculing her pretensions, making her feel the way Ivan had done when she dared to criticise the contract he had got her to sign? With him it had all been praise for her work at the start; only later had things sunk to a level of destructiveness that had had her on the verge of giving up.

'Carrie thinks they're all right,' she muttered, trying to extinguish the trepidation at what he might say next.

'Carrie?' His lips barely moved.

'My tutor when I was at art college.'

'She thinks they're all right?' There was a lift of the eyelids to show he had registered what she said and found it . . . amusing?

Jane drew herself up as best she could. So what if he did think her work was rubbish? 'I respect her opinion,' she forced herself to say. 'I'll get better if I work hard enough.'

He gave a harsh laugh, but at that moment she heard a hiss from the kitchen. 'Quick! Give me the lamp!' She reached up, tremblingly conscious of his vibrant, virile body only inches from her own, her fingers closing round the stem. 'Let me take it.' She gave a tug and he released his grasp. Conscious of the guttering flame and the smell of burning oil and the continued sounds from the kitchen, she made a hurried escape.

The light revealed a mess of bubbling liquid all over the wood-burning stove, the acrid smell making her curl her nose in distaste. He came noiselessly behind her.

'Leave it to me.' He pushed past her, then she watched as he reached for a cloth and lifted the pan off the stove in one movement. He swept the cloth over the hotplate and managed to clean it up, while Jane hovered with the lamp, feeling unexpectedly useless.

He finished the job, then threw the cloth into the sink. 'Why the hell are you living like this?' he demanded, straightening and turning, jaw jutting. 'I know it's romantic and all, but it's pathetic.'

She licked her lips, not wanting to fight but driven to defend herself. 'How dare you?' she managed. 'What right have you got to come breaking in——?'

'I was *invited* in.'

'By default!' she was stung to retort. 'Only because you'd got yourself into difficulties! What was I supposed to do? Let you drown?'

'Look, I don't want to fight with you.' His voice softened.

'Then don't. Just keep your opinions to yourself.' Jane was suddenly trembling all over, but she wouldn't let him upset her, and she swallowed hard before saying, 'I thought you had phone calls to make?'

He stepped towards her and the light she was holding shone more directly on to his face, making it glow and picking out every detail—the grooves on either side of his mouth, the tiny lines at the corners of his eyes, each separate black eyelash glistening in the light. She was tall, but he was almost a head taller and much broader. She felt overwhelmed when he came this close. She could see the muscles of his chest expand beneath the black jacket.

'You're right,' he checked himself. 'I do have calls to make. Have you only the one lamp?'

'There's a little one in my bedroom.'

He gave her a look of furious disbelief and his muscles seemed to distend even more. 'Bedroom?' he exclaimed. 'You mean you use an oil lamp in your bedroom? What if you fell asleep with it on? If it fell over during the night? Don't you realise you could set yourself on fire? This old place would go up like tinder.'

Yet another disparaging reference to her home brought a flush to her cheeks, but she forced it under control and said lightly, turning away, 'I've never really understood what tinder is.'

An exasperated exclamation made her turn back. 'Show me where your room is,' he demanded violently. 'We're going to have a long talk, you and I. Meanwhile——' he strode past her '—see if you can scrape a meal together out of this debris.'

He vanished into the dark in the direction she'd indicated, unaware of the outrage he'd left behind. But at least the tension abated after he'd gone. He was like a walking volcano, fire and flame, and all of it aimed in her direction. Nothing she had done warranted this ordering about and passing judgement, and if by talk he meant there was more to come she wished the night was over and he was gone. He made her feel small and useless.

She took extra care over preparations for the meal, all the while telling herself she was doing it for herself, not for him. But even so she got out the linen table napkins and matching crockery, registering that it was the first time since she'd moved in that she'd bothered.

She heard him moving about in the small bedroom before he came down to phone, and wondered why on earth she was allowing a complete stranger to roam around her house. No doubt there would be remarks about the contents of her bedroom next. She blushed when she remembered the furry hippo sitting on the pillow.

God, she thought, why should I care? Let him think what he likes.

The footsteps came down again, each tread creaking with his weight. It was odd to have another person in the house. Jane realised how much she'd missed having somebody about the place. But it had to be. She couldn't live in a shared house with a lot of other students any more. Those days were over, and the days of loneliness and dedication had to start.

She went into the conservatory to set the table, her nerves alert to the black presence only feet away. There was a battered pine table from some bygone age with enough room for six round it, and she placed a setting at each end, far enough away to keep the temperature down.

He was still on the phone, and she could see his black shape, crouched in silhouette, speaking rapidly into the receiver. He spoke with the same impatience he seemed to do everything else, and she was relieved his arrogance wasn't reserved just for herself. She forced her thoughts on to his beached power-boat—it seemed incredible to think that a man like him could have made such a stupid mistake. It should have brought him down a peg, but his confidence was obviously unshakeable.

She heard him raise his voice a little. 'Do that. As we arranged. Round about three-ish. And don't keep me waiting—they don't call it the North Sea for nothing.' He gave a suddenly humorous chuckle with that rich, musical sound from deep inside his chest Jane had noticed before, and it seemed to soften the sharpness of his orders. 'A lot of surprises,' he added as if in answer to some question. 'I'll explain when I see you.'

There was the click of the receiver, and she wondered if he minded that she couldn't have helped listening in to his side of the conversation. Despite having the manner of an autocrat he seemed to have a remarkably good relationship with the people he was calling. Nothing to do with me, she told herself firmly before the speculations could start.

'I think we can eat now,' she called, to forestall any further temptation. 'That is, if you've finished your calls.' Another thing she would have expected was a cell phone or something.

He rose to his feet, and she was mesmerised as he moved towards her on a dark tide of purpose.

Forcing herself to tear her glance away, she placed the casserole in the middle of the table next to the cold dishes she had discovered in his bag. There had been a torch there too among the edibles.

'This looks romantic.' He eyed the table with its pretty unglazed crockery, then lifted his head. 'Where do you want me?'

His blue eyes were less than innocent, a more suggestive meaning in the question, and Jane averted her face, quietly pulling out a chair. Crazy thoughts so lascivious that they made her skin redden were swarming into her mind, as no doubt he was aware, but she said in a carefully controlled voice, 'I saw you had a bottle of wine in your bag.

Maybe we'd better give it a miss if you have to drive later?'

He took his place opposite. 'I'm not driving anywhere. Somebody's coming to pick me up.'

His eyes were empty, giving no clue to add to this piece of information, and she wondered who but a wife would be at his beck and call. He'd said there wasn't one.

He gave her a silent glance from the far end of the table, and she could feel the power of his energy directed towards her, but without a break he was picking up their earlier conversation and said, 'So you're Hutton? I still can't quite get my head around that one. You'll have to give me time.'

'I don't understand,' she replied. 'You're talking as if you know me. Or is it Ivan you know? Are you a friend of his?'

'Ivan?' he queried.

'Ivan Clegg, the owner of the gallery I was with.'

'Ah.' His eyes emptied. 'What's your first name, Hutton?'

'Jane,' she admitted, wondering why he'd so adroitly changed the subject. 'What's yours?'

'I'm sorry. I've been thoughtless.' He reached into an inside pocket, and drew out a card, pushing it across the table, then watching her closely as she read it.

'Jed Mitchener.' She looked across at him. They were both at opposite sides of the perimeter of light, their faces lit as if in a painting, a moment out of time. And he was watching her with those clear eyes that seemed to see into her inner self. She placed the card carefully next to her plate. It bore a central London address and one in California, but no other information.

'You know what I do for a living, Mr Mitchener. Are you going to restore the balance by telling me what you do?'

Her glance was glued to his face and she saw the well-marked brows rise slightly, then two verticals appeared just above his nose. The blue washed over and around her in a glittering ocean. With a jerk of his head he growled, 'You're not putting me on, are you?'

Her eyes opened, but he seemed satisfied that her question had been innocent and said, 'What do I do?' He gave a curt laugh. 'You sweet creature.' He glanced round at the crystal room with the sea already surging back underneath it. 'Living like an innocent in your sea-house.' The idea made him chuckle, but he lifted his dark head and told her, 'You could say we're both in the same game—visual communications.' There was a quick, open smile, electrifying in its sudden brilliance.

Jane felt her stomach lurch. When he wanted he could switch on the charm in a way that sent out a measurable electric charge. 'Advertising?' She steadied herself. One of the professional persuaders, obviously. She couldn't help giving a dismissive tilt to her chin.

But he was shaking his head. 'Not unless you want to stretch the term out of all recognition.

This,' he said, looking down at the contents of his plate as if suddenly noticing there was a meal in front of him, 'is quite delicious. It beats me how you manage to cook anything in that old-fashioned kitchen of yours.'

'I like it, and everything works. And I like cooking.' Why had he changed the subject?

'How come they manage to let a place like this to the general public?' he went on before she could get back to it.

'Because it's really quaint, that's why. People like that sort of thing. But——'

He cut her off. 'It'd be fine for a weekend, perhaps. As a love-nest. Crystal and water, a water palace. But to live here all the time? You must be mad.'

'Thanks,' she clipped. Despite a flicker of annoyance she was distracted by the idea of a love-nest. As a notion it had a lot going for it. Dream on, she told herself firmly. She was here to work.

He leaned towards her. 'Come on, Jane.' Now it was he who wanted an answer. 'Why here?'

'I like it,' she defended. She wasn't gong to tell him about her mother—an artist to the very end of her life, but one who had never managed to separate it from family life so had somehow never achieved much—and her own determination not to fall into the same trap, but when he went on looking at her she admitted, 'I needed somewhere cheap, quiet, and preferably beautiful. Somewhere where I wouldn't be disturbed,' she added pointedly.

'Oh, I see. I've wrecked your evening!' He gave a chuckle. 'I promise I won't wreck your life.'

He got up. 'Where's that wine?'

She was still pondering over what he'd said when he returned, presumably having had to grope around in the dark to locate the bottle. He drew a knife out of his pocket and pulled out the cork-screw attachment. He seemed prepared for any eventuality.

She couldn't help saying, 'For somebody who was careless enough to sandbank their boat you seem remarkably efficient.'

'I've got that little fiasco to live down, have I?' He gave her a strange smile. 'Trust me. You'll get the whole story one day.' Before she could question him he raised his glass. 'Drink with me, Hutton,' he urged. 'Let's drink to our exciting future.'

'Ours?' Steadying herself, Jane picked up her glass. 'Yours may be exciting, but mine's not going to be. I can't afford the time.'

'What do you mean by that?' He narrowed his eyes.

'I promised myself I'd dedicate myself to painting. It's all I've ever wanted to do. All I can do. There'll be no time for anything else.' Carrie's voice urging her to make a choice came back. There can be no half measures, she had told her. You can be good or mediocre. If you want to be good, you have to give it all you've got. It was a recipe for life, and Jane embraced it whole-heartedly. She didn't want to have regrets later on like her mother and feel she hadn't fulfilled herself. And she wanted to be good. She wanted to be the best.

Now Jed Mitchener was on the other side of the table, his smile deceptively mellow in the lamp-light. He lifted his glass to his lips. 'To our future, and all the excitement our hearts desire.'

The meal was the most romantic Jane had ever experienced, but it wasn't because of the way he tried to talk to her. He didn't seem to be the type to go in for a lot of soft talk. It was something else. She watched him as he talked, trying to work it out. There was his aura of wealth, the sophisticated veneer paradoxically emphasised by his under-stated but obviously expensive clothes. On his wrist was the discreet lustre of a broad band of gold, and he had an air of having been everywhere and done everything. But underneath the civilised mask there was another man, one who was raw, physical, emitting a primitive energy, a sense of personal power like something barely tamed. He was clearly at home in the urban jungle, and she imagined him negotiating with unflinching skill the traps set by its cut-throat values and savage greeds.

But the romance that seemed to cloak him arose from a sense of something more.

It was connected to his uncompromising maleness, but as she felt herself succumb Jane knew it was more than that. It was a sort of mellowness, an almost feral sensitivity to mood. He listened to her and he responded. This attentiveness aroused a yearning in her soul she didn't know she had, spinning it out from some tightly coiled cocoon deep within, so that by the time they came to discuss the possibilities of locating some dessert in the unlighted kitchen she was completely under his spell.

It was as they got up to find the basket of late strawberries he claimed to have brought with him that she recognised she would have to exert all her efforts to damp her feelings down. For one thing, she still knew nothing much about him. He could be anyone. She didn't know his family. She didn't know who he really was and, snobbish though it might appear, it was that sort of knowledge that would have made her feel secure. She also revered hard work, and he seemed, to say the least, a bit of a hedonist.

Strawberries indeed! Summer was over. 'You're really decadent,' she accused, half joking but convinced it was true.

They had gone on the strawberry hunt together and were groping around at opposite ends of the counter-top in the kitchen with only the reflected light from the sea relieving what would otherwise have been unbroken blackness.

'Got them.' He seemed to surge towards her out of the night on a tide of desire she could imagine drowning in. 'Now what was that about decadent?' he murmured just above her head. Something sweet-smelling floated on the air. 'Open your lips,' he persuaded, his voice like black silk.

'No!' she protested, trying to ward his hand away, her nerves jangling at the sudden intimacy of taking the invisible fruit from between his warm fingers. 'Don't, Jed.' She used his name for the first time. It brought a new intimacy into the game, and she backed away, full of nerves, banging her elbow on a corner cupboard.

All the sympathy she got was his soft laughter out of the darkness. 'Trust me,' he persuaded. 'Trust me, Jane.'

She melted against the door where he couldn't touch her. 'I do trust you,' she admitted, astonishing herself with the sudden truth of it, and when he seemed to be waiting for a reply she went on, 'It's just that I haven't time for distractions. I mean, I can't paint and—well, you were asking why I was living here alone, and it's all part of the same thing. And we're so different,' she finished lamely.

It was strange, standing in the dark, waiting for his reply. His voice seemed to wind its way right inside her body, giving it a positive physical charge. She was wild about his voice. Speak to me, caress me with it, she beseeched in silence.

He seemed to come closer. 'We are different, yes. But there's nothing wrong with that.' She sensed that he'd moved closer still as if picking up her trail out of the darkness. 'But, Jane, we are alike, we both inhabit the same sort of world. We both need beauty in our lives.'

She felt a strong hand take her by the elbow and when she tried to draw back he pressured it softly then started to guide her back into the other room.

'Let's pace ourselves,' he suggested softly. 'There's no need to rush. We've got forever.'

Her breath caught. 'Forever?' She ran a hand through her hair. What on earth could he mean? 'B-but you've ruined my schedule!' she stammered at the thought of what the night might hold. 'I'll never do a proper day's work if I'm up till dawn. I need to be in bed by ten.'

She faltered when she realised what she'd said, but he didn't make any stupid, suggestive remarks, instead asking, 'Is it this tutor of yours who makes you drive yourself so hard?' His eyes were softly probing and never left her face. She couldn't answer at once, watching fixedly as his beautiful tanned fingers moved among the strawberries, picking out the best and pushing them across to her.

Eventually she shook her head. 'I want to do it. Mum and Dad were painters. I know Mum wanted to be much more than just another landscape painter, but when Dad got sick of being saddled with a wife and child and upped and left us she had to go out to work, and somehow she never fulfilled her dreams.' She hesitated, but Jed was still giving her all his attention, and she went on, 'Maybe some of her ambition has rubbed off on me. It's as if something drives me.' She wondered if he understood. 'The college seem to think I can make it,' she went on, 'and this seems to be the only way to do it.' When she glanced up next she thought she detected a hint of criticism in his eyes, and his words seemed at first to confirm it.

'You *are* ambitious,' he remarked.

'What's wrong with that?' she sparked back.

'Nothing,' he said promptly. His smile gleamed across at her and he said unexpectedly, 'On the contrary, I like to see naked ambition.' He smiled like a panther contemplating the hunt. 'It's honest. It's strong. It excites me.' His voice dropped. 'I like glossy, ambitious, hard-boiled women, the type who never break. They excite me.' His eyes were like flecks of steel.

Jane shivered. 'You make it sound cold and hard.'

'It doesn't have to be. It can be the hottest thing there is. It's survival. It should make you feel alive all over.'

She didn't like the sound of this. All those women—they sounded too competitive, too grasping, and he didn't seem to mind! She could just imagine them all over him, competing with a thousand schemes because he was such a catch. 'I still think it sounds nasty and egotistical, and it's not what I meant.'

'But if it's what you want, you've got to see it for what it is.'

She shuddered. This wasn't how it had seemed in those long-ago summer days when her girlish water-colours had brought encouragement from her mother, nor did it sound like this when Carrie talked of success. Jed's idea of it sounded frightening, destructive, a power-house of insatiable needs. A world she didn't want. Then she laughed. 'I may be ambitious, in fact I am, as far as being a good painter goes. But it shouldn't carry over into ordinary life. And I hope it doesn't! You couldn't say I'm the glossy, hard-boiled type.'

He agreed—too readily, she felt. 'But you're just not trying,' was his unexpected rejoinder. And as her mouth dropped open he went on, 'If you were you wouldn't be scruffing around in a pair of old shorts and threadbare T-shirt you must have had since you were twelve. You'd have an expensive pair of jeans, a designer top, your hair trimmed, your nails polished and a beautiful painted-on smile. And,' he added for good measure, 'you would never, ever find yourself living in a place like this.'

'Don't you mean to say a "dump" like this?' she bit out, cut to the quick by the vivid image he conjured up. She didn't mind frankness, but this was brutal. And he didn't even know her. But then it was all true. She wasn't smart. She had let herself go, living out here by herself, and she knew she was impossible about practical things—a complete mess. So what was new? She refused to let him see how hurt she was and instead lifted her chin to give him a defiant stare.

'If I'd meant "dump" I'd have said so.' He regarded her severely from across the table. 'It's pretty here, it's romantic, but it's total threadbare living, and anybody with an ounce of true ambition would write it off in favour of a place with all the material necessities for running a successful career.'

'You mean one crammed with all the visible symbols of success, I suppose? One designed to impress? Well, in your world they might,' she went on scathingly, 'but in mine we consider it rather vulgar to be so ostentatious.' She bit into a strawberry to stop her voice from going on and on.

Of course she would prefer a modern house to this rackety old place, but it just wasn't possible. Now she sounded about a hundred years old, as if she'd never had an extravagant impulse in her life. But it was said now, and he could think what he liked.

'Hutton...' he pushed his plate to one side '...you're a type.' When she dared raise her glance she expected to see that by now familiar thrust of the chin, the steel-eyed, disparaging glance, the blackness of thwarted will, but to her astonishment his expression was almost relaxed. In fact, more, he was looking extremely pleased with life, as if he'd been the recipient of an unexpected prize.

The conversation after that slipped on to other more general topics, and he started to tell her a little bit about his American childhood. 'I was brought up in a real rough part of LA by foster-parents, and after the usual kid stuff of running away and getting mixed up with the local wild bunch I somehow got myself sent out to work off my high spirits on the ranch of a very remarkable old lady. I guess you could call her my Carrie, my mentor. She taught me a hell of a lot, and she taught me the one thing I thank her for above all else.'

Jane waited.

'That was a kind of appreciation, a love for beautiful things.' He considered her upturned face, then turned so he was focused on the little ceramic figurine on the coffee-table. 'I know you understand that too, about art and music and natural beauty. Despite what I said about this place it really is very visually stunning—all this water and crystal. But I guess for you it's sort of inbred into you, as natural as breathing and eating. For me it—well, I tell you, this sort of thing was not on the agenda for kids like me.'

He got up and came round the side of the table. 'Hey,' his voice dropped an interval, 'I don't mean to get heavy about it. I just want you to understand what it means to me. Beautiful things, why I go after them.'

He fixed his cobalt eyes on hers and slowly reached down and touched the top of her head.

She felt her back arch like an animal as the thrill of his caress shot through her. She reached out wildly, trying to look as if she was beginning to clear the table. But Jed wasn't fooled. He picked up one of her hands, turned it, then placed his lips gently in the palm.

Abruptly he broke away and paced over to the window with his back to her. Jane felt shaky and couldn't work out why. Was it because of what he had told her about his past? It certainly put him in a different light. She could almost understand his drive, after a boyhood like that.

But there was something else too. It was as if he was trying to tell her—no, prepare her, for something. But what? Was he going to make some revelation? A confession of some sort? But he just wasn't the type. Confession implied hesitancy, guilt even, but despite his sensitive antennae he was basically the caveman type, without a shred of guilt in his soul. And as for hesitancy! Her palm burned where he had kissed it. Might as well ask the tides to hesitate in their headlong thrust up the beach.

As if to confound this impression he was hesitating over by the window, turning to look at her at last and saying lightly, 'Listen, Hutton, you've got to get your sleep. I understand. And I don't want to waste your day tomorrow. You go and tuck up, and I'll let myself out when it's time.'

'I can't do that!' she exclaimed. A mixture of different feelings confused her for a moment, clarifying in the knowledge that she couldn't allow a complete stranger to roam around her house while she slept, even if he did have the most seductive voice in the business. 'I'll have to show you how to find the path to the causeway,' she excused. 'It'll be pitch-black out there.'

'I happen to have a torch.'

'I know. I saw it.'

Their glances locked, his as if to say so what do you want to make of that? hers an open question which she put into words. 'Do you always go about so well prepared?'

'You forget, I was on board a boat. Even if it is just a gin palace it has basic equipment on it,' he said quickly.

'Did you suspect you'd be trapped somewhere till late?' she queried without thinking. As soon as the words were out it sounded ridiculously suspicious, as if she was accusing him of something.

'I thought you of all women would applaud prudence and forethought?' he remarked drily.

'Is that how you see me?' Jane ran a hand over her face. 'Prudent?' How could he say a thing like that when she'd been heedless enough to allow him in in the first place? But they seemed to be sparring, unexpectedly fixed in attitudes of opposition, some secret like a black rock separating them. 'I think I must be tired,' she muttered, searching for an excuse.

'Then go to bed. I'm used to looking after myself.' His eyes roamed mockingly over her face, registering the fact that she had no intention of doing as he suggested. He stifled his impatience. 'Look, I'll fetch you a blanket. Snuggle up on the sofa and if you want to get your head down for five minutes you can.'

It seemed too hard to resist, because he had obviously made up his mind that that was what she was going to do. She would humour him, she thought. But she certainly had no intention of going to sleep until he was well and truly off the premises.

CHAPTER THREE

'BEAUTIFUL things . . .' the voice seemed to murmur in her ear. 'I love beautiful things around me . . .' Jane groaned and twisted. There was something soft digging into her cheek. What . . .?

Her eyes blinked open and memory scudded back. With it came the fact that the room was swimming in sunshine. 'Oh, no!' she exclaimed, half aloud. 'The time! My schedule!'

She rolled over and came face to face with Mr Snooks, the fluffy pink hippo she'd had since her fourth birthday. 'Thank you for waking me.' She patted him, reverting briefly to childhood, then she dragged herself from under the duvet.

What time had Jed Mitchener left last night? Despite her good intentions, once he'd wrapped her in a blanket and settled himself safely on the other side of the room she had eventually nodded off, waking only when she found him bending over her, shaking her gently by the shoulder.

'I'm leaving now, Hutton,' he had said, 'but I'll be back.'

She had tried to insist on showing him the way to the causeway, but he wouldn't hear of it.

'And have you trying to find your way back here in the dark? Not a chance.' He had bent and dropped a light kiss on the top of her head. For a moment her senses were on fire again, but he straightened at once, saying, 'Let me see you upstairs, then I'll make sure the lamps are out before I go.'

She remembered staggering a little, the blanket catching round her feet as she stood up, but he hadn't put out a hand and he hadn't said anything else, but she could feel his eyes on her as she groped her way towards the stairs.

Later, lying in bed, she heard the downstairs door snick shut and the receding tread of footsteps on the wooden jetty that linked the house to the foreshore. Then quiet. Not even the cry of a lone night bird to break the silence. He had gone.

Grabbing a quick breakfast and a large mug of black coffee, Jane made her way into the studio, stopping short as she opened the door. Her two big paintings, the ones she was working on at present, were on adjoining walls, and a group of others, completed but waiting for a final assessment before she showed them to anyone, were stacked against the third wall. They were massive pieces, only the brown canvas backs of the finished ones visible, but she felt instinctively the hands of a stranger on them, tampering with them, taking possession of them.

Perhaps tampering was too strong a word. She tried to be fair, but she couldn't get away from the fact that Jed had touched them, moved them, taken them over no matter how briefly. Tamper wasn't strong enough for the way she felt, for it was like last night again when he had brushed aside her objections and gone prowling through to have a look for himself with an uninhibited lust to see for himself that had all the force of a physical assault.

She imagined the scene—his black shape in the golden light, bending to the lamp on the floor, for even he would have needed both hands to swing the eight-foot canvases away from the wall, and then what? She imagined the quick blue eyes judging and assessing, and again the raw silence as he came into the room where she was waiting.

Irrational though it was, she felt as if it had been her own body he had touched, secretly taking possession of it in the darkness as if he had a right to such knowledge. She shivered as the feeling of forced intimacy engulfed her like a black wave.

This is totally irrational, she told herself, and tried to remember that Jed had only fingered a few inanimate bits of canvas. But it didn't work. The feeling of assault haunted her, and she paced about, unable to pick up a brush, tormented by what he might have thought.

He hadn't admitted to liking her work, or even understanding it, but then he hadn't said he didn't like it either. The lack of response made her desperate to know the truth, even though she told herself again and again that it didn't matter a damn. He wasn't an artist, a critic, what did he know? But she felt his verdict would have been a reflection of his deepest feelings about her, signalling what he truly felt, for weren't her paintings a part of herself, the important unseen part, the part that had nothing to do with the surface of physical looks or fashion flair, but they were everything, simply everything, to do with the person she really was inside?

Last night she hadn't been able to judge whether it was to see her or her paintings that Jed had promised to return, for it had all passed in a romantic blur, his sky-blue eyes hinting at horizons she longed to explore. Now it came down to one thing: work.

Placing her coffee-mug on the work table and dragging on a blue fisherman's smock she sometimes wore when things were going to get messy, she caught up her abundant hair in its usual ribbon and riffled through the tubes of acrylic in a businesslike manner. Yet it took the best part of the morning to get into her stride again. Disruptions of any sort upset her. Her temperament was the kind that needed the discipline of routine to allow the ideas to flow, and she cursed Jed Mitchener under her breath for invading her life and turning her emotions awry.

The sea was back under the house as it had been last night, booming incessantly and making the foundations shake.

He returned as promised, appearing like an oceanic force of nature himself halfway through the day.

The first indication Jane had that he was near was the roar of a motor outside the window, and when she went to look she saw the knife-edged shape of a power-boat, black as doom with a comet trail of foam behind it, disappearing out of sight. Whoever was manhandling it through the swell had sent it arcing out into the river before she could make out the details, but then it was roaring back, its occupant evidently having decided which window she was at.

The engine was cut to a feline purr and, face pressed to the glass like a prisoner in a tower, she managed to angle her gaze sufficiently to make out the shiny black hull as it lifted and slapped on the turbulence of green water below.

Today he was wearing a tight black T-shirt, the muscles of his manly chest outlined as if by a master draughtsman. The dark glasses were back in place, bronzed jaw and black hair so right, so complete, the look of raw masculinity so blatant that Jane felt her breath catch. Then he saw her and raised one hard-muscled arm aloft while he mastered the boat against the swell.

With what looked like practised skill she saw him jockey the craft towards the seaward side of the house and disappear from view. Surely he's not going to try to come ashore? she thought. A man who crashed a much bigger boat on the sandbar would probably try anything, she realised, rushing from the studio and into the conservatory. She flung open the french doors and went out on to the balcony.

He wasn't alone. A companion, a grey-haired man in a peaked mariner's cap, was holding a coil of rope in the bows, but even as she watched Jed gestured him aside. She saw him take the wheel while Jed, judging the distance with athletic precision, leaped for the ladder and in a trice was climbing up towards her as the boat powered away.

'OK, come on,' he said, without any preliminaries. 'He's going to do a circuit, then come back for us.' He gripped her by the forearm, overwhelming her with his sense of urgency, so that she was a pace towards the top of the ladder before she realised what was happening.

'Wait a minute!' she protested. 'What do you mean, coming back for us? I'm not going down there!'

'Yes, you are. Come on—stop arguing. Tide and time and all that. If we don't get aboard now we'll miss our chance, and I've got to be back in town tonight.'

'But—look here.' She tried to pull away. 'Take your hands off me, Jed Mitchener!' She might as well have saved her breath, for he was already bundling her towards the top of the ladder.

'Don't waste time. I said we had some things to do. I'll explain when we're on the boat.'

'What boat? Just leave me alone, will you?' She began to struggle, but his strength far outbid hers and she felt the full power of his hard thighs crushing her against the rail. For a moment she was conscious of his hot maleness, obscenely intimate, pressuring against her and drawing from her a surging response, carnal and unbidden, before she managed to twist away, the humiliation of a blush betraying a primitive response that exactly matched his own.

His arms, wrapping her against him, slid with a slowing pace down her sides to her hips, swivelling her to face him again, his mouth lowering until it was only inches above her own. There was a hiatus as if he was as much taken by surprise as she was, then she felt both powerful hands encircle her wrists.

'Put this down,' he murmured, taking the paint-brush from her nerveless grip.

She had even forgotten she was holding it. It slid from between her fingers and fell on to the wooden slats of the balcony.

'I have to clean it——' she protested.

'I'll buy you a hundred new ones,' he promised. 'Come on.' His voice had descended to a husk as if her touch had taken something from him, and they swayed together until the roar of the power-boat broke the spell. He seemed to shake himself, then all at once he was the invincible marauder of a few moments ago.

Still resisting, Jane somehow managed to find herself perched on the top rung of the ladder. She gave a fearful glance below. The cockpit of the black boat was bucking like a wild thing in a spray of silver foam, while above the powerful male figure blocked her escape. 'I can't do it,' she cried, overwhelmed by indecision.

'Yes, you can. I've got you. Take hold of the sides.' Firmly he placed her hands on each side of the ladder. 'Down—go on!'

Instinctively she obeyed the note of command in his voice, trusting him to guide her down to safety. It was obvious he was used to taking charge. As he was blocking the way back she had no choice but to do as he demanded.

He followed at once and dropped into the bottom of the boat beside her. 'That was easier than it looked, wasn't it?' His dark brow furrowed with triumph as he took over from the older man and gave the engine full throttle. Jane was jerked back into the passenger seat as the boat bounced across the open waves into mid-channel.

Her hair flew out and her words were whipped from her lips, but thankfully they began to slow almost at once and the bows, thrusting upwards under the power of the engines, dropped so she could see the white hull of *Barbarossa* lying ahead.

When Jed had called it a gin palace, she noted drily, he hadn't been exaggerating. It was enormous, with a wide white sundeck bigger than the average dance-floor.

He cut the engine almost completely and brought them skilfully alongside. 'Jed, I can't do this,' she told him reproachfully when she saw they were supposed to board the bigger boat. 'I'm supposed to be working—I really am. I thought you understood that?'

'I do.' He turned and said something to the man in the cap, who picked up a coil of rope in the bows, and when they were level stepped from the smaller boat to the bigger one and linked them firmly together. Jed dealt with the stern line and when all was steady held out his hand. 'Come aboard. I told you we had much to discuss.'

There was nothing for it but to obey. Presumably this was meant to be a sort of thank-you for her at first grudging hospitality last night and, grinding her teeth with annoyance at the arrogant way he had hijacked her, Jane climbed over the gunwale on to *Barbarossa*.

Jed followed close behind, guiding her below out of the wind.

It was like a hotel suite inside, with nothing nautical about it. There was plush white carpet everywhere in the main saloon and much chrome and white leather, with a bar and fixed seating around what looked like an Italian marble table inlaid with gold mosaic. It seemed flashy and overdone, not to her taste at all, and it further confirmed her opinion of Jed Mitchener as a caveman type, as impressed by glitter as any primitive tribesman. Maybe I should bring out the coloured beads in order to barter my freedom, she considered.

With no pretence at being a willing captive she flung herself down on one of the leather seats and glowered up at him. 'I had a dream about you last night,' she said icily. 'It must have come from when we were talking about the Roman causeway just before you left, because you were dressed like a senator or something in a white toga, and you were in charge of some barbarian outpost of the Roman Empire.'

She frowned. Maybe the story needed editing, otherwise he'd get the wrong impression, but she'd seen him in the dream as the sort who would be at the top of any organisation he deigned to join—he exuded that sort of authority. 'You had the task of supplying the slave market,' she told him drily, 'picking and choosing the ones to be shipped back to Rome. "You, you and you," you were saying—typically arrogant.' She didn't tell him she had been one of the captives, stepping forward in obedience to the senatorial nod of the head.

'Are you trying to tell me I'm being high-handed?' His lips were curving humorously, but the concealing sunglasses made his mood ambiguous.

'You?' she exclaimed in mock astonishment. 'As if!' She bestowed a look on him that would have turned an ordinary mortal to stone, but he didn't even flinch. With an exaggerated sigh she asked, 'Perhaps you'll be kind enough to tell me what all this is about? Or is it just a thank-you for last night?'

'I fully intend to tell you everything, but not before we've had a civilised drink and I've dealt with my skipper.' Jed had been positioned in the saloon doorway, and now he climbed out on to the deck where the other man was busy. Snatches of conversation floated down to her, and while the heat was off Jane took the opportunity to glance round.

It would make a satisfactory if luxurious prison, she concluded. The portholes, eye-height all round, were too small to climb out of, and the only way out was the hatch through which Jed had exited. The radio he would carry on board to comply with safety regulations must be on the bridge deck, and apart from a sleek galley area there were only several closed doors leading off into what she supposed were the cabins. Everything gleamed with luxury, and there was an expensive hush, with only the faint buffeting of the waves and a slight rattle from the anchor chain reminding her that she was actually at sea.

Jed was back in a minute, accompanied by the skipper. 'I'll have coffee, then,' the man was saying, 'and then get back.' He was introduced as Gerard, and then the two men talked engines while the kettle boiled.

By now Jane was suffering in silent fury. What had he brought her here for? It was tantamount to piracy, forcing someone on to a boat against his or her will. When the other man left she would give him a piece of her mind! She thought furiously of the painting she had been engrossed in, remembering how she'd broken off in mid brush-stroke at the unexpected sound of the engine. Her present predicament was her own fault. She'd only intended a quick glance to satisfy her curiosity. If she'd ignored him maybe he would have gone away.

Any illusions like that were dispelled when Jed turned his black gaze on her a few moments later. The other man had left in the smaller boat, the whine of its engine dwindling with frightening rapidity and making her isolated state the more immediate. Jane felt her eyes raise fearfully to the dark force surging towards her.

'I want to go back,' she whispered, unable to express the anger of a few minutes ago. 'Please, Jed.'

'In a while.' He lowered his powerful body on to the bench beside her. 'I said I'd come back for you, but I'll begin at the beginning.'

Her breath was hurting to be released now that he was sitting beside her. He made her acutely conscious of that sleeping sexuality she had succumbed to from the first, and she shivered as she felt him shift against her, rocked by the movement of the boat. A hot longing to feel again the contact of his body against her own spread itself like molten fire along her veins. She was fire and ice, held in suspension, fearing yet yearning for his next move. But he seemed deep in thought, apparently oblivious to the effect he was arousing, his mind on something else.

'I told you last night I liked beautiful things,' he began after a moment, 'and I've been a collector ever since I could afford to buy whatever caught my eye. Back home——' he turned to her '—in California, that is, I've got the beginnings of an interesting collection of fine art—mostly new young painters.' He made that dark mellow sound that made his laughter all the richer. 'I figured that if anybody needed help it was artists just starting out. And besides, some of them would turn out to be sound investments for the future.'

Jane didn't say anything. Her mind was in a whirl, the more so because every time the boat lurched they were thrown against each other, an extra torment that he didn't even register. Her body was glowing with desire, tingling for a more complete contact with him.

'OK? So are you asking where you fit in?' he demanded, turning the dark glasses suddenly in her direction.

She managed an untruthful nod, scarcely able to register the question, with her lips, her breasts, her thighs burning in a way she had never experienced before. The wild thought entered her head that she was beginning some sort of fever, that there was a purely physical, viral explanation for her sensations, but she knew she was deluding herself. If there was a fever it was all due to sexual chemistry.

Unaware of her turmoil, Jed went on, 'I was in London early this summer, and while I was there I chanced across a gallery in the West End which had on exhibit some of the finest paintings I've seen in a long while. It was love at first sight. I'm like that—instant reaction. All or nothing. I have an immediate visceral response to things which I trust implicitly.'

The hidden eyes seemed to hold hers, then he was lifting his head, turning, shifting his position before continuing. Now, with the change of position, she could feel the muscles of one of his powerful arms brush lightly against her left breast, and when the boat lurched again he seemed to press more forcefully. It caused her nipples to tauten with excitement and she scarcely dared to breathe.

He went on talking, while she tried in vain to digest what he was telling her.

'When I collect I'm fanatical,' he admitted. 'I simply have to have what I've set my heart on. I make no apologies. Sometimes, though, it's darned inconvenient. Like wanting to possess the works of this painter called Hutton. The gallery owner wouldn't help. I told him to get me everything he'd done. But there were difficulties. I assumed he was trying to up the price by making them seem scarcer than they really were.'

He turned to her and his lips were drawn back in a smile. 'His assistant kept telling me how uncooperative Hutton was, making out he was some sort of eccentric, reluctant to let his paintings on to the market. I decided that if he wouldn't play ball I'd track him down myself, parley with him, see what he could offer me straight from the studio, let him name his price. As I said, I wasn't bothered about that. I was willing to let him set his own figure. I wanted everything he'd done. At any price.'

The boat lurched again and she was distracted by the brushing of her breast against his arm, and when he shifted again at the same moment she became trapped like that, burning with the need to have that powerful touch caress her aching flesh with more deliberation.

How can he not be aware of what's happening? she wondered feverishly, trying in vain not to miss a word. He continued, 'It was difficult to track the old guy down. I was told he was a recluse living out in the marshes. At least, I was told *Hutton* was a recluse... Imagine how I felt last night when I beached the boat, deliberately, I might add, and managed to storm the citadel... Where was the old man with the Van Gogh beard?'

She felt him lift up one of her hands, freezing as he trailed a finger experimentally over the inside of her wrist.

'Some old man,' he murmured, 'some beard!'

'You really thought that?' she asked, momentarily distracted. Then, as his trailing finger continued to explore her wrist, she became conscious of shooting stars bursting sensationally over her entire form in a way that had nothing to do with what he'd just revealed.

'When I saw you standing there looking down at me like a princess, I thought, So the old guy's got a beautiful daughter. It appealed to my romantic streak. I decided there and then that she was going to benefit in some way too, even if it meant giving her father a stipend. Believe me, I love those paintings I bought. They were worth any price he cared to ask.'

Jane gulped. He liked her work? No, he didn't like it, he *loved* it. She felt dizzy for a moment. Following her previous line of reasoning, it must mean he liked her, then? She pulled herself up. Even if he did like her work, she reminded herself sharply, he was no expert. Just a rich man with a fanatical zeal to collect things.

Through eyes still hazy with desire she looked at him in surprise. He must be very rich to be able to indulge his whims to the extent he was suggesting. The forefinger of his right hand drew ever-diminishing circles on her wrist, whorls of pleasure, sending her senses spinning into a vortex of desire.

'So there it is, Hutton,' he finished, husky-voiced. 'Now you know I didn't pile up on the sands like some hot-headed idiot. It was a deliberate ploy to get something I was desperate to have.'

'So you want to buy some paintings?' she managed to croak. 'But——' she bit her lip '—I'd be happy to sell, only the time isn't right. You see, nothing's really finished yet. Not in this new series. All the previous ones were sold.' She lifted her head. 'How many did you get?'

'Only two. There were eight more. They'll come on to the market some time. I'll get them all eventually.'

Jane tried to think straight. 'The thing is, I need my work to be seen.'

'It'll be seen,' he assured her. 'I'm not planning to lock it away in some vault. I'll get it shown in all the top galleries. Not for sale, but seen, talked about, applauded.'

'The two of them?' she queried.

'And everything else you paint.'

Jane swallowed. 'I can't allow that.'

She felt his head jerk to look at her. 'What are you saying?'

'If you're willing to wait I can let you have a look at them, but I can't let you have them all.'

'You're refusing to sell?'

She shook her head. 'Not exactly. But——' She tried to clear her head. 'I have to build up a body of work. I need to have them around me. I'm not just in this for the money—I'm working something through. Each painting is like a sentence in a novel. I need to have them near me. All of them. Until it's over.' She didn't expect him to understand. How could she? He was a businessman, not an artist. The quality of his silence proved she was right.

She groped for words. 'You see, it's like Carrie says, I have to build up a body of work. A one-off *tour de force*, a painting that fetches thousands, is all very well, but it's a very masculine way of looking at things. It's not for me. I don't operate like that. What matters is the consistent quality of what a painter does, maturing over time.'

'No box-office smash?' Jed asked in a voice that was dangerously quiet.

She nodded.

'You're wrong,' he came back harshly. 'One hit can make you. Just as one flop can finish you off.'

There was a pause in which she could hear only the rubbing of the anchor chain against the stem of the boat, yet there was an immense, brooding silence from the man beside her that was as pregnant with foreboding as any shouted command.

He had been thwarted badly, she could tell, but when he did at last bring himself to speak his voice deceived by its very control. 'I'll tell you something, Hutton, and I'm going to say it once only. I thought my quarry was a guy, not a girl. I flew in to buy him up. Nothing's changed except the pronoun. I'm going to buy *her* up. You. Get it?'

'I don't——'

'And before you try to marshal any objections let me tell you something else. I haven't been thwarted by anyone since I got out of short pants. Further, when I say I'm going to buy you up I mean just that. I'm buying you now. I'm a collector. And rattle your chains all you want, you're my prize purchase.'

CHAPTER FOUR

A FLAME of fierce sexual need leaped between them before Jane felt a chill dread send daggers of ice into her stomach.

'Now just you look here, Jed Mitchener, you may think you can call the shots where you come from, but you're not getting me in your trap!' She was on her feet at once, eyes flashing, a storm of emotion welling up as she turned to face him.

'Sit down, Hutton,' he drawled. 'I haven't finished.'

'I will not sit down! Who do you think you are to order me about? You——' She grabbed at the first word that sprang to mind. 'You caveman!'

His expression was still concealed behind his dark glasses, but his lips tightened and he reached out one powerful hand, and though she stepped back the movement brought her sharply up against the Italian table, making it easy for him to haul her into his grasp despite her kicking and fighting like a wildcat. He was still sitting down, and he overbalanced her so that she sprawled across his knees. The muscles of his chest were like granite against the plush fullness of her breasts, and she felt a quiver of desire shoot through her from heel to head.

'You black devil, Mitchener!' she gasped as his hands began to slide over her bottom in an unashamed caress. She struggled wildly, but he continued to knead her soft denim-clad form to a high pitch of sweet yearning. 'Don't, don't,' she cried, feeling the betraying pull of her emotions melting her limbs against him. 'Please don't, please, please don't.'

Her cheek was resting against his hard, clean-shaven jaw, and it involved only the smallest fraction of movement for him to bring his lips closing possessively over her own, then she was swimming in a sea of flame, desire to plunge yet deeper sending her resistance spinning into oblivion.

He dipped again and again into her yielding mouth, his tongue tasting the honey of her lips in a maelstrom of sweet plunder, then she felt him roll her beneath him on the long leather bench, stretching out her arms above her head and bending again and again to her prostrate form. His body was hard and demanding, forcing an open display of the desire she had so far managed to conceal. Now it was an open secret, with her responsiveness plain to see.

But his words rang in her ears, taunting her with all their male pride, making her determined to resist. He might have released a storm of longing, but it didn't alter the fact that he saw her as just a purchasable object on a par with any other commodity that took his fancy. But she was not to be used like this. She tried to swivel her head, to avoid the lips that sought feverishly for her total submission. But she felt his mouth drift instead to her neck, the mounds of her breasts displayed by the fingers pulling at the neck of her T-shirt. She struggled, turning and jerking this way, then that, while the blood pounded in affirmation at his touch.

He seemed to lift his head out of a blurred dream, and with a harsh exclamation pulled her up so that her face was crushed against his chest. He allowed her feet to swing to the floor.

'Damn it, this isn't what I want.' His eyes squeezed shut and he shook his head like a boxer coming out of the ring. His chest expanded as he breathed deeply in and out, establishing control over his frightening virility. He pinned her arms distrustfully to her sides. 'You're not going to fly at me again with your claws out, are you?' he growled.

Jane shook her head in protest. 'I didn't!' She was as dazed by the sudden turn of events as he seemed.

Jed went on holding her by the arms as if he didn't quite believe her. 'OK, Hutton. Now tell me what really upsets you.'

'Just leave it, will you?' she muttered, avoiding his glance.

'Caveman?' He cocked one black brow. 'I did hear that, did I?'

'You did.' She kept her face averted and studied the saloon floor.

'You by contrast being so fine and sensitive and artistic, I suppose.'

'I didn't mean it like that,' she muttered.

'Do you know what you did mean?'

She held her tongue. He was playing with her, surely able to hear her heart thumping through the obscenely masculine chest that was pressing against her breasts. His body was burning up like a bonfire, and she wondered in what hell's kitchen he usually dined. He sure as heaven wasn't going to dine on her.

Taking her by surprise, he rose abruptly to his feet and went to sit on the opposite side of the cabin. 'Listen, Hutton. Forget the last thirty seconds.'

'Was that all it was?' She raised her hazel eyes, her stare glazing over. Had he been counting the seconds to see how long it took to persuade her to surrender?

'Forget it, I said. This is a business proposition. What I propose is, I take you back to town and set you up in a studio, then you'll be able to paint undistracted until you establish yourself.'

'Set me up in a studio?' Jane couldn't help the scathing laugh that escaped. Her chin rose. 'In the good old days before the women's movement you'd have suggested setting me up in a penthouse flat, I suppose. How we move with the times!' Her furious glance washed over him, without effect.

'I said a studio, and that's what I meant. There'll be nothing like the last few seconds. It'll be purely business.'

She shot him a disbelieving glance. 'I'm not leaving the beach house.'

He gave her a ferocious glare that silenced her and leaned forward, dominating the confined space with the blackness of his will. 'You mean you'd rather struggle on in that God-forsaken rented shack, out of reach, out of touch, unknown, a recluse, when you could be at the centre of things, seen, known, fêted by those who count? I thought you said you were ambitious?'

'You don't know what I mean by ambition, obviously,' she said as cuttingly as she could. 'I just want to be free to paint as best I can.'

'Don't you believe you have real talent? Is that it?' he demanded.

She stared at him, her eyes darkening. He saw the doubt in them at once. 'Listen, you know you can hack it. Isn't that what your tutor told you? Somewhere in that muddled head of yours you know you've got what it takes. But it needs somebody to manage it for you, to take away the stress and strain of daily life. I'm offering to do it. No strings—just a controlling say in where you exhibit. Believe me, I've done business with the top gallery owners in the game, here in Europe and in the States. I'll make life easy for you. I'll smooth your path. All you'll have to do is be successful. Are you afraid? Do you think you can't do it?' He reached across the table and fixed her with a look of fierce accusation. 'Are you scared that if it's made so easy you'll have no excuse left for failing?'

'No!' Jane was pulled to her feet by the force of denial. But he was watching her, pitiless, refusing to allow her an escape.

'Come on, Hutton,' he said softly, 'admit it. You want an excuse to blow it. Stuck out here you've got all the trappings for failure. That's why you chose it. Why else would you choose to live like a nun in the middle of nowhere?'

'It's not true! It's not!' Even as she spoke Jane was aware he had hit on one of her darkest fears. But in a whirl of sexual arousal and fear at being manipulated by him she was also aware of a sneaking fascination at the thought of the power he seemed to command. She put up a hand. It was impossible to think straight. Somehow, bound up with it all, was a knot which would take some time to unravel, and it was how his interest in her work fitted in with the way he'd just kissed her. He seemed to be denying a connection. No strings, he'd said. But if they were separate, if it was only love for her paintings that interested him, what then?

She brushed a hand over her eyes. Suddenly she had a most piercing headache, as if the dazzle from the sea were penetrating deep inside her skull. She closed her eyes to ease the tension. 'This isn't fair, Jed, and you know it,' she said quietly.

'It's fair,' he said, unaware of the conflict that held her in its trap. 'I've put you on the spot. What's fairer than that?' He was referring to their business deal, as he liked to put it. 'You can take the chance while you've got it. Prove you can make it. Or you can chicken out. But I can tell you something—I'm not going to let you chicken out. So the choice comes down to facing it. Choice and no choice. You're on the line, Hutton. And I'm not letting you get away.'

'I don't know what megalomaniac scheme you have for making me paint to order,' she muttered. She knew she had lost. She couldn't think straight, and there seemed to be no escape from the blind force of his will. To be able to paint without having to bother about routine daily chores? To have her work exhibited in the top galleries? Why wasn't she dancing for joy?

'Do you always do business like this?' she asked in a whisper. 'I've been put through a wringer, and I'm not sure who, if anybody, has come out the other side.'

'You'll find out soon enough, I promise you. Come on, I'm going to take you back. We've plans to make.'

The biggest practical problem, as Jane saw it, was to find a suitable studio space and to get her paintings transported safely to it. She put it to Jed on the way back to the marina where the boat was kept. There was even a slight look of triumph in her glance as she outlined the problem, as if defying him to find a solution that would satisfy her.

He considered her words at face value, ignoring the emotional undertone, and asked for specific dimensions and details to do with light and access.

She was as exacting as possible, feeling that if she put him off now it would save time and trouble later.

'As well, you'd better understand I have to finish the two paintings I'm working on at the house, and there's no way I can break off before they're done. I'd never be able to get back to them again.' She made it sound final.

Jed took her seriously and asked how long she would need, and she scowled and asked, 'How long is a piece of string?' and he sighed and said,

'Ten days. I'll give you that much. So make sure your bags are packed.' He consulted a tiny electronic diary pad and forced her to fix a date there and then.

What she didn't tell him was that she had paid a full three months' rent on the beach house with the last of some money she'd earned in the summer, and felt she could regard it as a get-out if the new arrangement didn't work. She would leave some things behind, so that if or when the worst came to the worst she could escape back to the life she was leaving behind her and carry on as if nothing had happened to interrupt its uneventful and satisfactory flow.

'Mr Mitchener,' she said as she eventually climbed on to dry land, 'you really like to call the shots, and I'm not used to fitting in with anybody else's plans——'

Jed interrupted with raised eyebrows. 'I can see that, Hutton. But have you considered whether it's healthy to be so wrapped up in yourself?' He gave a dismissive turn of the head, so missed the way her mouth dropped open.

'If this is going to work at all,' she said as forcefully as she could, 'you're going to have to realise that I need to be alone.'

He turned back, his face impassive. 'You'll be alone.' He gave a dangerous smile. 'You'll be as alone as any human being could wish.'

Then he released the line that had held the powerboat against the quay. 'There's my chauffeur up there by the clubhouse. He'll drop you back at your place. See you on the tenth.' He lifted one hand without looking back, and the gleaming white palace slid majestically away from the wharf.

Jane watched the ever-widening gulf of water that separated them until he was near the marina exit. Then she turned. He hadn't looked back. Well, damn him. What she had wanted to warn him, but dared not bring herself to put into words, was that she didn't intend to be seen as his latest sexual acquisition.

The picture she had built up of him was consistent. He was an obsessive collector, both of things and people, and it didn't seem to bother him that there might be opposition to his lust for possession. Recalling his promise about being alone, she gave a shiver. It had sounded horribly like a threat, a portent of explosive days ahead.

* * *

When she got back she had a good hard look at herself in the wardrobe mirror and came to the conclusion that she didn't look too bad, despite what Jed had implied about her scruffy appearance. It was difficult to tell how she would compare with the glossy women he seemed to prefer, and she wondered what she would look like if she ever had the time to spend at hairdressers and manicurists—not, she vowed, that she would ever be lured into adopting that sort of empty lifestyle.

Before she went to bed that night she spent longer in front of the mirror than was usual, and even dabbed a little face cream on some imaginary wrinkles. Her eyes were large and dark and long-lashed and gave her wistful sort of look which Jed Mitchener must have mistaken for a willingness to be dominated. He should have taken the trouble to look further, she surmised, for even she admitted that her mouth was wilful and her chin, if these things added up to anything, was firm and resolute.

Of course, she thought cynically, it might have been her nearly waist-length hair that had confused him. It was a sun-streaked Nordic blonde that when she did it properly could, so she had been told, look like the fly-away tresses of the Botticelli Venus, the one rising from the sea on a cockleshell with one hand modestly covering her sex. There was a warning for Jed Mitchener in that, she thought with a grim smile . . . and a guiding beacon for herself.

* * *

Over the next ten days Jane painted like a fury. It was the best therapy she knew for emotional conflict, and she truly believed she had scarcely given a though to what Jed Mitchener was planning for her. But early on the tenth she remembered what he had said about packing her bags, and she ran round the house throwing together a few essentials, all the while half believing that the whole event was a dream, or he would have changed his mind, or something—anything, except that he would actually turn up and whisk her away.

The paintings, nearly finished two weeks ago, were now gleamingly complete, and she felt ready for a break, lingering in the first euphoria that came with finishing a piece before the habitual depression settled and she started to imagine how much better she could have done. If only, she thought. If only. Two words Jed Mitchener had probably never uttered in his life.

Today the tide was far out across the sandbanks and the river looked like a harmless blue pencil line between the ochre channels. Jane was sunning herself on the balcony when she saw three figures, one in front and two following with what looked like some sort of hand-cart, marching along the headland towards the jetty. Nervously she brushed a hand through her hair and stood up. Her fingers fiddled with the neck of the burgundy velveteen dress she wore for the occasion, and by the time Jed and his entourage reached the house she was biting her lips nervously, determined not to show

how suddenly frightened she felt at the prospect of what lay ahead.

'Got your gear?' was the brisk question with which he greeted her.

'Listen, Jed, I don't think this is a good idea,' she blurted, surprising even herself at this belated attempt to deflect the thrust of his intentions. 'You see, I need peace and quiet, routine, all those dull things you couldn't possibly provide. I mean——' she blushed, angry with herself for being so transparent '—I don't need this.'

'I promise I'll provide all the dullness you require. What you do need is to nurture your talent before it's deflected and destroyed by the hassle of making a living. You need a proper studio and you need to be able to get out to galleries and talk to people who know about art. That's what I'm offering. Make it as dull and routine as you like. We won't even meet, if you think it might prove too exciting for you.'

She felt her heart give a flutter of protest, but her lips framed an acquiescent yes. 'Is that a promise?' she whispered.

Jed held one hand out and brushed her palm with it. 'A definite promise,' he vowed with an air of bleak foreboding.

'Where is this—this studio?' she managed to ask. Expecting some word from him since their last meeting, she had had nothing but an ambiguous silence she had been afraid to question in case it broke the spell.

'I told you, didn't I? You'll be at my place in town. You'll have all the space and solitude you need.'

He gave a violent jerk of his head. 'Time's short. Let's get your stuff loaded and you'll see it soon enough.' He gestured to the two men with the cart. 'Show them where your bags are. We'll have to make special arrangements for the paintings. I assume they're finished?'

Stung by his slave-driver attitude, Jane gave a toss of her head. 'I said they would be, didn't I?'

Secretly she was appalled at the prospect that had just opened out, for surely he didn't expect her to *live* with him? She had believed him when he had promised the three things she needed—space, solitude and a percentage from the sale of her paintings to live on, and now she told herself that if it was a lie she could turn right round and come back here.

Unaware of her qualms, Jed gave her a brief smile which she took as a sign of approval that she had met her deadline, before shouldering his way inside the house with his usual air of having no time to lose.

After she'd shown the men what things to load she went to find him. He had located her new paintings straight away and was standing in front of them, his face darkly brooding, a forbidding cloak of silence round him that didn't lift even at the sound of her footsteps.

She hovered in the doorway, her mouth suddenly and inexplicably dry. What was she worried about? she asked herself. Did she think he was going to change his mind this time and declare that she had no talent after all? Nerves prickly with apprehension, she waited for his verdict, but when he swung round he gave her a raking glance much like the one he had bestowed on the canvases, a glance that clearly labelled everything under the one word 'mine'. Jane flinched at such a crude display of his inmost thoughts.

With his intent look on her there was no chance to escape when he prowled slowly towards her. He came to an abrupt stop, and she felt sure he was going to reach out and touch her, but despite the fact that he was only a pace away, and so close she could scent the unmistakable tang of citrus and bay, he didn't raise a hand. Instead the blue eyes feathered over her upturned face for a moment, dizzying her with the potent message they contained, suggesting that it would take little to strip the mask to reveal the primitive man beneath. Then as if it had only been a dream his expression of glittering mastery was substituted by one that conveyed a glacial detachment. 'I've a lot to do today, so let's move.' He thrust on ahead out of the room, leaving her to stare after him for a moment before gathering her teeming senses into some sort of order and following him out.

She caught up with him. 'Aren't you assuming a lot?' she demanded.

His lips set in a straight line. 'Such as?'

'I mean, that you can fix everything?'

'I usually can. Try me.' His blackness came down more firmly than ever, a dark challenge, not to be swayed.

She watched him walk away down the jetty after a brief word with his men, and then it was all movement with the things loaded and the cart being pushed erratically back over the path towards the causeway and then the bumpy journey across the island to the bridge, where a black Range Rover waited. The men climbed into the front, while Jane and Jed took the seat behind them, and it was with a last flurried glance over her shoulder that she allowed herself the dangerous luxury of putting her future into the hands of Jed Mitchener.

When the Range Rover at last nosed into an alleyway in one of the narrow back streets of Soho, the gates at the far end swung open at the touch of an electronic safety device. Then they whispered into a courtyard dominated at one end by what Jed told her was a restored Georgian print warehouse and at the other by the black glass walls of the modern main building.

The men got out and started to unload her paintings, while Jed guided her into the foyer. Jane felt her worst fears confirmed when she realised that they were in the headquarters of a film production company. Jazzy red carpets and a lot of chrome and open-tread staircases greeted her sight, and a woman of the glossy kind Jed had already alluded to sat behind a reception desk with an array of technical hardware on it that would have done justice to the cockpit of a jumbo jet.

On seeing them she pressed some invisible buzzer and the lift doors sighed open. Jed, with a brief word to say he would be down shortly to deal with his messages, came brooding towards Jane like a malevolent force.

'Let's go up.' The lift conveyed them both with silent precision to an upper floor. How many floors? she wondered, confused by Jed's silent proximity. Then he stepped out ahead of her, guiding her across a tiny vestibule to a solitary door with its own entry-phone.

Cautiously, not quite convinced she should be doing this, she followed him inside. It was her private apartment, he told her, where she could come and go as she pleased—or not, if she preferred hermit-like isolation. Food could be arranged without any trouble, she only had to ask.

She gazed round, not saying anything. If he expected a lot of approving 'ooh's and 'aah's she intended to disappoint him. Did he believe, she thought furiously, he could impress her by this display? Her first impression of the apartment was that it was overdone. After the makeshift conditions of the beach house there seemed to be too much of everything.

Yet the more she looked, the more she grudgingly admitted that his interior designers at least had taste. A melding of soft blues and greys, very restful to the eye, provided the main colour theme throughout, and she couldn't help but approve the clean lines of the galley kitchen with its impressive array of equipment, and the simple, practical luxury of the shower-room. Plenty of cupboard space everywhere, she noted, and in the sitting-room three or four comfortable armchairs, with, finally, a lovely double bedroom looking out over a city-scape towards Whitehall and the Houses of Parliament. She poked about in all the cupboards and pressed switches on and off.

There was only one thing wrong as far as she could see. Where was she supposed to paint? On the table in the kitchen?

She turned to him, the question already apparent in her eyes. But before she could frame the words he jerked his head impatiently. 'Follow me.'

He had been watching her with the close-eyed stare of a predator gauging the reactions of its next victim, and she was relieved when he turned and led the way to a spiral staircase she had assumed gave access to an attic bedroom. He ascended with his usual impatience, and she hurried to keep up, arriving breathlessly at the top, only to stop with a little gasp as she reached the landing.

His glance was fixed unflinchingly on her face with a look that commanded her complete and immediate surrender.

'It's very nice,' she managed to admit. Then she felt her eyes brim before she could stop them. She couldn't help noting the disappointment on his face at her grudging inspection of the accommodation he was offering, but her distrust of the situation had got the better of her and she'd refused to show any signs of gratitude.

Now her response was genuine. 'It's quite perfect,' she admitted.

Then she stepped into the middle of the high arching chamber which was to be her studio, and gave a little spin for joy. 'Nobody's ever offered me such a perfect place to work in!' She turned to him. 'I suppose I didn't really believe you!'

To her humiliation she found her eyes, already brimming with the unexpected generosity of his offer, begin to overflow. 'Tears of happiness,' she explained, dabbing at them with her fingertips.

'You idiot. Stop it.' Jed put a hand on the back of her neck and gave her head a little stroke.

'I didn't believe you,' she whispered. Her face lifted to his before she could stop it, but he moved away as if not wanting to be accused of exacting anything that could be seen as payment. His expression was impossible to decipher.

'So, there it is,' he said as if something had been finalised. 'Settle in now. I'll come back to hear your comments later.'

After he'd gone Jane stood in the middle of the room and threw her arms in the air for sheep happiness. Wasn't she the luckiest girl alive? How had he managed to get everything so right?

She went over to the pulley that worked the blinds and saw how she could adjust the light coming in from the clerestory windows high up. There was such a lot of space, masses of it, and already she was visualising the sort of canvases she could attempt now there was room.

There was a studio table, long and capacious enough to take all her equipment. There were wall sockets for spray-guns, a sink for cleaning—she turned both taps on and off. And if she got bored in this wonderful eyrie there was the marvellous visual show of London spread out below the windows.

Only one thing marred her contentment that evening as she unpacked and started to settle in, and that was a niggling little sadness that she hadn't shown her gratitude enough. Really, she had been mean, and Jed's expression had shown her that he was hiding how upset he felt.

She hoped to be able to thank him properly before she went to bed, but, by the time Big Ben struck ten, he still hadn't reappeared, so reluctantly she decided to call it a day. If she was going to make use of her brand-new studio she wanted to get a good start in the morning.

She walked round it one final time before turning in. To say she was overwhelmed would have been an understatement. She had wanted to fault it—him—had expected to find everything wrong with it, half hoping, with a perversity she feared to analyse, that it would be so bad she would have a valid excuse for upping sticks and leaving first thing in the morning. Jed was, after all, a caveman with no understanding of the needs of an artist, but now she was willing to eat humble pie.

Her feeling of warmth was allowed free play as she took a leisurely shower, then sank gratefully into bed. Sighing and stretching, she was drifting in that never-never-land before the threshold of sleep, relaxed enough to give free rein to her current good opinion of Jed Mitchener and admitting at last that she was enjoying the process, when there was a sound like a door opening in the next room.

She froze, senses on alert, even the hair on her head standing on end for a moment, until she recognised the dark bulk of the man looming in the doorway of her bedroom.

His sudden appearance and the shock of realising that he actually had a key to her apartment put to flight in an instant all the pleasant thoughts she had been having about him.

It had been a trick after all! A business arrangement, he had said. No strings attached!

But if that was so, what on earth was he doing, moving through the shadows to her very bedside?

CHAPTER FIVE

FOOTSTEPS trod purposefully towards the bed, and Jane felt her body go rigid. She restrained the impulse to keep her eyes open and forced them shut, making her breath sound deep and rhythmic as if she were asleep. Maybe if she did it well enough he would leave.

The sense of his male presence in proximity to the bed ordered her to look up, but she struggled against the temptation, all her senses aroused and reaching out like antennae, straining to pick up the slightest message that would tell her where Jed was and what he was doing. Her hearing seemed to sharpen so that she could hear the soft in-and-out of his breath, her nostrils dilating at the hot scent of him, the light touch of the cotton duvet over her naked skin taunting her with the thought that its flimsy protection was all that separated them.

A soft moan escaped her lips before she could stop it. She tried to turn it into a sleepy sigh, burying her face deeper into the pillow. There was a movement from behind her, and prickles of alarm ran up and down her back as her nerves readied themselves for his touch. She waited. In her turmoil she forgot about her breathing, and it was only when she heard the rustle of material as Jed pulled back the duvet that she remembered and managed to give a sigh of pent-up breath, restraining only barely the impulse to gulp in torrents of oxygen in compensation.

Now she could feel cooler air flowing over her naked back where he had exposed it to the night. Still she continued her ruse.

There was again a long silence from above and behind.

Now her senses were at screaming pitch, straining for every change in the atmosphere that would tell her of his intentions. Subtly, numbingly, came the seductive scent of the particular brand of lemony French aftershave he used. It wafted over her with a haunting familiarity, reminding her of their first meeting when they had talked together in the darkened beach house. It aroused associations that made her long to turn, to open her arms to him, to respond to what was in her heart, but they were impulses that had to be crushed out of existence if she was to survive and not become just another addition to his collection, with no will of her own.

Now she was being driven to the furthest limits of control by the overpowering tension emanating from him as he watched her. The very air seemed to vibrate. She knew he was looking down at her with those eyes which could travel the range of blues from steel to forget-me-not in a moment, that he would be able to pin-point every curve of her body in the purple haze seeping in through the window, the busy nightscape below emphasising the silence of the room and their proximity. She could almost feel his glittering scrutiny silver over her recumbent form, touching and tasting its curves and hollows from her bare nape to the silky rotund shape of her bottom, surely visible beneath the fold of her coverlet. Her nerves tingled, sensitising the exposed surface of her skin, every cell craving his next move.

He made no sound, and she tried to guess what he was thinking and how long she could keep up this pretence and why, oh, why he didn't turn and release her from this longing. A question hammered in her head, and she longed to swivel up to him and demand to know what it was he wanted, standing there in silence in the night, not touching, but looking, voiceless with some empty-hearted intention towards her.

With a shudder she felt his hand come down on to her shoulder. It was as inevitable as fate, feather-soft, and by contrast her emotions seared her from the roots of her hair to the very centre of her being with an input of unbridled desire. With a welling of emotion she could do nothing to quench she knew she had been longing, yearning, even seeking it. Her lips emitted a muffled groan and she half turned, but her lids lay heavily over her eyes, for she had still not entirely relinquished her pretence.

She felt his fingers touch with butterfly lightness the curve of her shoulder, the nape of her neck, and, forcing her breath to flow smoothly and deeply as if in the throes of sleep, she moved slightly, like a dreamer.

But his fingers continued to smooth as lightly as a warm breath down the length of her arm, pausing intimately over the back of her hand, then returning again to her shoulder, changing their path to follow a dizzying route over the small soft muscles of her back. She could feel him pause at each vertebra, making whorls of sensation that sent her limbs into a liquid heaven of bonelessness as if the bed had turned into a cloud and she was being borne will-lessly away.

She pressed the side of her face more deeply into the pillow to conceal the flush on her cheeks, feeling a sudden mellowing heat in the pit of her stomach that told her she was no longer in control. But now she could feel both hands smoothing her naked back, and the rasp of his breath telling of the intensity of his own arousal, while his hands slipped lower, cupping around the full softness of her buttocks in a movement that made her long to turn and stretch her slender legs so that she could more easily offer herself.

But she knew she must not. To surrender to him would be the end. And surely soon he would stop? If he failed to exact the response he wanted, his lust for sexual domination would peter out and he would retreat. All he wanted was to show he had absolute control over her, and if she denied him that he would lose interest and this torturing manipulation of her senses would come to an end.

Another low moan was dragged from deep inside her throat as she felt the marauding fingers taking further liberties, seeking out her most private places, one hand teasing the nipples of her breasts between forefinger and thumb, the other sinking deep inside the shadowed V of her thighs with a subtlety that almost deceived her into thinking it was only her imagination after all, and still she fought to lie still and to keep her eyes firmly shut, while her breathing, though deeper, portrayed the very image of sleep.

He was turning her slowly, slowly rolling her on to her back. She felt her limbs expand and soften as they would have done naturally during sleep, this faking of oblivion her only defence.

Her head was hammering with the denial that she could be made into one of his whims, his purchases, to be sucked dry of everything she had then thrown out with the rest of the jumble from his collection the way a small boy would discard yesterday's toys. Yet now she was displayed before his eye like an ornament, a piece of living sculpture on the white pedestal of the bed, while he assessed her with the silence of a connoisseur.

Now he was slipping the duvet in a silky torrent down the length of her legs until nothing lay between herself and his gaze. All her senses were alight with anticipation, and the blood roared in her temples while inside she cringed at the way she was conniving in her own defeat, for now her legs splayed as he had arranged them and she waited, quivering, for what he would do next.

'Stop pretending, Jane, you know you want me,' she heard him mutter from below her waist, and something soft which could only have been his lips pulled so deliciously at her thighs that she could scarcely contain a cry at the spasm of pure pleasure that shot through her. She cringed even further inside herself, detaching her mind from what was happening to her body as if by doing so she could save herself from admitting she desired it too.

'Jane, Jane,' she heard him husk, 'you can't be asleep through all this.' Then his lips closed over her skin again, pulling it into little peaks of sensation that made her want to cry out in a passion of desire. Her mouth had opened of its own volition, yearning to feel the touch of his lips, his fingers, and, as if reading her mind, she felt him reach up and press a thumb against her upper lip, tracing its bow and sliding two fingers deep inside to massage the soft opening that yearned towards him.

Now the blood was beating a hard rhythm in every pulse to keep time with the dark need that was making her respond to him. She dared to move a little to allow him greater freedoms, murmuring as if in a dreamlike delirium, even half believing that the velvet night had itself conjured up this apparition of desire beside her bed.

'I want you,' she heard him growl hotly into her ear, his voice rising in a hoarse whisper driven by sheer animality to press his demands. 'Tell me you really want this—show me.'

She was in a furnace, on fire with the need to feel him even more intimately teaching himself her body's symmetry, groaning with the ache of longing, yet even now when she arched, quivering, towards him, she did so as if moving in a voluptuous dream.

'Show me,' he insisted, 'speak to me. Tell me with words.' His voice rasped urgently against her brow, and she could feel the hot breath over her skin, tantalising and shocking with the private sharing of a mutual fever.

Her mouth opened to take his with a sudden jerk of instant hunger, an ache to have it, his lips, his mouth, his tongue, sundering her resistance, but he wrenched his hot, moist mouth from hers before the spiral of need could spin them simultaneously out of control. 'I must hear you say it, Jane. Say you want me.'

Her head fell back as her neck arched to make further contact with the sheathed steel of his muscles as he began to press over her, and without knowing it her hands slid inside his shirt to explore in ever-increasing wonder the perfection of his shape.

'No, Jane, no.' Hard fingers gripped her chin. 'Look at me, open your eyes,' he demanded. Rough with passion, he forced her head hard back against the pillow, and at last, reluctantly, only half aware of what she saw above her, but, acceding to his demand, she felt her lids flicker open. Long lashes veiled the vision of his face leaning above her, but she shivered at the blaze of desire in eyes that were probing feverishly into her own.

'Now tell me you want me in words I can understand.'

She was aware of his body poised above her own, tensed to such a pitch of desire that the smallest hair's breadth was capable of sending him plunging deep into the mystery of her being whether she wanted him to or not. But his words had riven through the hypnotic state she was in, resounding again and again through her mind like a voice full of doom. There was an escape from the natural conclusion of events which he was offering her, even though her faked sleep had not saved her. Words, or the non-utterance of them, were the passport to safety. Her shadowed pupils dilated beneath his gaze.

'No,' she breathed in a broken voice.

'Tell me yes,' he commanded with a groan.

'No, oh, no,' she protested, quivering with need.

'You want me, say the words to me,' he insisted in a ragged voice.

'I hate you,' she said on a sob, while her hips arched convulsively against him.

'Say it,' he commanded again.

'I don't want you,' she cried as convincingly as she could. 'No! Leave me alone.' If he didn't stop at once she wouldn't be able to help herself.

With a tearing asunder that sent rivers of anguish swelling through all her senses their bodies separated. Now she could see the black sweatshirt, the pelvis-hugging jogging pants, the outline that betrayed the pitch of desire he had been driven to, and as she felt a cry like a traitorous cry of desire rush into her throat Jed gave a harsh curse and wrenched away from the bed. He was at the door in a trice, then there was a movement and the door slammed behind him.

'Oh, God.' She was shaking, her whole body aflame with unsatisfied desire, her breath rasping in and out with a frenzy of longing. If he hadn't left then she wouldn't have been able to stop herself. The ache for him was unbearable. It made her fling herself upright, rolling off the bed in a manic wish to throw herself after him, naked though she was, but she stopped midway towards the door when she heard the outer door click shut. No, no, she warned herself, don't do it. Keep away from danger, and thank God for a reprieve.

She flung herself down on the bed with a despairing sob. She was trembling violently with a chill that swept over her like sleet.

It had been a revelation to discover she could be driven by animal instincts, by pure desire, acting in this mindless way and so rapidly stimulated to such a frenzy of longing like never before.

She lay back on the bed, the coverlet slipping half off as she waited for a sound that would tell her Jed was returning. But at the behest of some strange, honourable code of his own, he was absenting himself, despite the blatant arousal of his primitive instincts.

Next morning Jane dragged herself late and irritable from the knotted sheets where she had tossed and turned until the early hours. Determined to put Jed right out of her mind, and convinced that once he had managed to stop himself from fulfilling his sexual urge he wouldn't bother to try again, she assembled her painting equipment and considered the sort of canvas she might work on next.

It was really too soon after completing her other series to start straight away on something new, but she felt that if she didn't try to plunge into work at once she would torment herself into madness with fantasies she knew it would be folly to permit.

There was a silence and coolness in the solitude of the studio. Like the beach house, it was a sort of virgin territory, away from all temptation. Yet, ideal though it was, she couldn't settle down to work. Every unfamiliar sound had her turning startled eyes towards the door, and she spent too long standing at the big windows looking down like a captive on the neon sights of Soho, her mind tormented by half-repressed imaginings.

The internal phone on her work bench alerted her, and she tensed as she picked it up, waiting for the voice she knew and concentrating on its initial sound in order to gauge his mood.

But he was bland, businesslike, asserting a need to hurry as he was, once again, in a meeting. 'Come down at midday,' he said tersely.

'What if I say no?' she managed to reply, subconsciously reacting against being ordered downstairs like a servant girl.

'If you don't come I'll have to come and fetch you.' The line went dead, leaving a mood of menace in the air.

Slowly she replaced the receiver and put her fingers to her lips. Already she was beginning to burn all over at the thought of seeing him. Moistness in her groin shocked her. He was a caveman. She'd seen that from the start, but so what? She didn't have to crumple at his feet, did she?

She would argue the whole thing out with him when they met, putting him straight on a few basics of good manners for a start. If necessary she would get him to promise to leave her alone. It wouldn't harm to remind him that all he'd said he wanted from her was the right to some of her paintings in return for helping to manage her career.

Another thought came to mind and she bit her lip. There was, as he himself once said, much to discuss.

To see him ranging across the scarlet carpet towards her, handsome as sin and as darkly dangerous as the devil, momentarily swept everything else out of her mind. But with an effort she reminded herself that if life was to go on they would have to find a way of working amicably, or at least, if that wasn't possible, coolly together. It would mean the temperature would have to descend a good few degrees down the scale.

To lay the ground for what she wanted to say she greeted him with a glacial expression. His own response wasn't much warmer. He scarcely glanced at her. 'Let's go,' he said abruptly.

'Where?' She dug in her heels, resisting the automatic guidance of his arm on her elbow.

'Lunch, of course. Or don't you artists eat food like ordinary mortals?'

Jane averted her face at this gibe and didn't bother to reply beyond murmuring, 'I can't spend too long.'

'Started a new work already?' he probed, his eyes alighting on her downturned face.

She glanced up at him through her lashes, then dropped her gaze again. 'I'm planning something, yes,' she hedged.

She heard him give a small snort. 'We'll soon see, won't we? I can't say I've done much work this morning.'

She knew he was blaming last night, but she pretended otherwise. 'You should organise yourself more effectively,' she returned.

From the evidence of one brief look round the place she realised he was heavily involved on film production, but in what capacity she had no idea. It astonished her that she should have failed to register basic details such as this, but everything had happened so quickly after his initial appearance, and she hadn't thought to ring him after he left, being too absorbed in work, but it made her wonder if it had been one of the things he had told her, only half heard, during that first night when she had nodded off out of sheer exhaustion while they waited for the tide to turn. Time enough, she thought, trying not to lean into him as he took a firm grasp of her elbow.

'We'll drive, even though it isn't far. I find it less troublesome,' he told her, sending her ahead of him through the swing doors.

They climbed into an unobtrusive small city runabout whose only distinguishing feature was its smoked-glass windows. They gave everything outside an unreal colour, making even the trees and the tubs of flowers outside the shops look artificial.

She noticed how pedestrians peered in at them, as if trying to make out the features of the celebrity inside, and she curled her nose at this obvious vanity of Jed's, as if he thought he was famous enough to have to go to such lengths.

When he parked he slewed the car across the yellow lines and left it there. As Jane got out she looked back and pulled a face. 'Aren't you bothered about being clamped, or do you imagine you're immune to such things, unlike ordinary mortals?' she mocked.

He jiggled the keys in the palm of one hand as he came towards her. 'The restaurant will see to it for me,' he told her with a cool smile as he brushed past.

She said nothing, but followed him into the dark entrance of the Wardour Street restaurant, wondering if she would ever get the better of him.

He was obviously a valued customer, and they were shown to an intimate alcove where a line of waiters jumped to his slightest command. To be fair, he didn't betray any of the arrogance she half expected, but nor did he for a moment let anyone encroach beyond a certain clearly defined level of intimacy. It was his unconscious air of authority, she supposed, that kept people in line. It seemed more marked now they were out in public, reflected back multiplied in the faces of everyone who looked his way.

She felt a strange sense of privilege to be seen dining with him. If he had started out in life as just a street tearaway the years and his iron will had put that world firmly behind him.

'So you managed to work this morning? What admirable dedication,' he remarked, soft-voiced, as soon as the waiters left them alone. 'Perhaps you're tougher than you look.'

She flinched a little, the heat already beginning to rise at the nearness of him. He gave her a sultry look which lifted the temperature even higher.

'Mr Mitchener——' she began, hoping the formality of her manner would send things back to freezing again, but he interrupted.

'Come on, Janey, there's no way we can pretend it didn't happen. Drop the pretence.' He gave a dark chuckle. 'You had me fooled at first last night, but I've been wondering since whether it was all fake from beginning to end.' His eyes probed her expression, and she fought back the blush that had started to rise at being found out.

'I don't know what you mean,' she said stiffly, 'but if we're to go on like this we ought to establish some ground rules.'

'Well?' he prompted.

She gulped. Was he agreeing so easily already? 'Well, first,' she said, after a pause, 'my apartment. I thought it was sacrosanct.'

'I agree. I shouldn't have come in like that. But I was worried. I finished late last night, but not too late. It was still a civilised hour to come calling. But when I rang up there was no reply.' He frowned. 'It crossed my mind you might have——' His frown deepened. 'Is that your only rule?'

Jane tried to guess what he might have been about to say, but it was no good guessing. 'I didn't hear the intercom,' she admitted. 'I must have been in the shower or something.'

'So? Go on.'

'Well, what exactly is our arrangement? I mentioned that I'd shown some work at a gallery this summer, the one you bought those two paintings from, but there's a contract. It's rather awkward.'

'Tell me about it.'

She frowned. 'Maybe I should have told you before, but everything happened so quickly.'

'I intended it to,' he told her. 'If I'd given you time to think about it you'd have backed down. Now tell me about this contract.'

'I was offered it shortly before I left art school. It seemed amazing enough to be noticed by one of the important galleries as it was—I mean, being completely unknown. So I didn't look too carefully at the small print.'

Her fine-boned features were serious now and she turned her eyes up to him for help. 'You see, Ivan—that's the owner—said he wanted an exclusive right to my work for the next year. But when it came to sales he paid only a fraction of what he'd said he would. At first I thought he was only able to get a small sum for them. Quite by chance I discovered that in fact he was being offered much more and was pocketing the rest. When I asked him about it——' she flinched '—he was really vile.' She swallowed, trying to shut out the dreadful scene that had ensued.

It hadn't ended there either, for Ivan had pursued her with demands for more work, insisting that she was breaking her contract and liable to end up in court with huge barristers' fees if she didn't hand over every painting she did.

Jed's lips curled. 'It fits,' he told her abruptly. 'His assistant told me he could get more work but that it would cost me more than double what I'd paid for the first two. I accepted it because—well, you know that side already. Now I know why he couldn't deliver and had to keep putting me off.'

'I thought I could sit it out for a year, living on a shoe-string, then, if he couldn't do anything with the ones I painted in that time, perhaps one of the other galleries would take me on,' she explained.

'Then I chanced along and you saw a way out.'

Her head shot up. 'It wasn't quite like that. I admit it must have seemed as if I jumped at your offer.' She frowned. No, that wasn't true—she had had qualms, still had, but to him it must seem otherwise. 'I hadn't really thought it through,' she added in confusion.

He gave her a cynical smile. 'No, my dear, of course you hadn't.' Icicles seemed to hang in the air. But he tensed his shoulders and leaned back, thoroughly confident. 'Don't worry, I still believe in your painting talent, even if I've had to revise my opinion about you.' Jane's pupils enlarged. 'You're as willing to further your career in the time-honoured way as any starlet on the casting couch. So what's new?'

She had risen to her feet before she could stop herself. 'No! It's not true!' she exclaimed. 'I won't do that!'

'Sit down. I don't like scenes.'

His voice was so clipped that she obeyed without protest.

'But it's not true,' she whispered urgently, conscious of one or two looks being cast in her direction. 'You know it's not.'

'Baby, I know nothing of the sort. All I know is what I've seen. The deceiving virgin in the crystal water-palace, waiting for the prince.' Jed gave a harsh, humourless laugh. 'Very pretty. I'm a romantic. I applaud it. But don't expect me to believe in it. You're as hot for me as I am for you, but you'll give only enough to keep me firmly on a string. But you needn't worry, I'm a man of my word. You can put your career in my hands. I'll groom you for stardom and you can trust me to do the very best for you. But that's got nothing to do with after hours.'

'After hours?' she queried.

'Come on, Hutton, wise up. You know exactly what I mean. Nobody, not even dedicated little you, can work all the hours God sends. And then what? You want to play, like any normal young woman. And my conviction is you want to play with me.'

An ocean of blue was washing over her, engulfing her senses in confusion until she struggled to the surface, fighting for breath. 'When we first met,' she hissed, 'you called yourself a collector, and so far I've got no reason to dispute that. But you should understand one thing, Mr Mitchener. My paintings may be collectable, but I am not.'

His derisory laugh sent tingles of ice up and down her spine. 'But I told you too that when I want something the devil gets into me and I can't control myself. And, Hutton,' his voice resonated with a return of last night's primitive desire, 'I want you. I want your eyes, teeth, lips, tongue, skin, every single golden hair on your head, every particle of your beautiful body—every atom...' he paused '...of your lascivious soul.'

His ironic blue eyes held hers, and she felt the betraying tide of scarlet, the very colour of desire, swoop up her body in an unmistakable sign of affirmation. Yet her senses were not so assimilated to the marauding power of his will that she couldn't find some resistance, and she felt her spine stiffen.

'No deal,' she whispered. 'As I said, I'm not collectable.'

Jed smiled comfortably. 'We shall see, my dear. We shall see.'

CHAPTER SIX

JANE made it clear that once she started work on her new series of paintings her time was her own. In the settling-in period of the next few days Jed respected her need for solitude, but every evening when he knew she had to take a break his black velvet voice would come whispering over the intercom, inviting her for a drink with the rest of the staff.

So long as she knew there would be other people present she dared to risk these impromptu meetings, and indeed she welcomed a break from the punishing isolation of her work, especially as the film company crowd, despite their self-obsession, were a witty lot, and their quick-fire *badinage* was fun as well as to some extent keeping her up to date with the outside world.

It was on the third or fourth evening when she went down that she discovered something about Jed that set her mind in a whirl. At first she told herself it wasn't true, then she remembered that first lunchtime when the restaurant staff had made such a fuss over him. It should have been hint enough, but then she'd been living outside the mainstream recently, otherwise she would have recognised the name Jed Mitchener straight away.

The first hint came when she went into the hospitality-room where everybody met after work. A group of account executives were over by the bar, and she went to join them.

'Here, seen this?' asked one of them. He thrust a glossy magazine into her hands. 'Another pretty picture of the boss.'

One of the secretaries jostled to have a look. 'Oh, isn't he gorgeous?' she sighed. 'Nearly as devastating as in real life.'

Jane went on staring at the double-page spread as if she couldn't believe her eyes. She was vaguely aware that the conversation around her had gone on to something else. She skimmed the accompanying article, then forced herself to go back and re-read it more slowly.

Film producer Jed Mitchener, it said. Her Jed? But why hadn't he told her? His lack of vanity in not making something of it was quite a shock. Most men would have been only too keen to draw attention to something like this. She couldn't work it out. Suddenly she saw him in a new light. The famous Jed Mitchener. Mr Modesty, she thought wryly. But where had she been hiding? Why hadn't she realised who he was? It was because of this quiet life she'd been leading, but then she had to, didn't she?

She felt a twinge of hurt that he hadn't mentioned who he was, but probably he thought she knew already.

She tried to join in the gossip that was going on, but secretly she pondered over this lack of vanity. It showed a side of him that didn't fit with the image she'd built up of a pushy, go-getting, somewhat shallow creature, glorying in the glittery trappings of success.

It was a shock to find out now that he was behind a host of international film successes, films even she had heard of. His handsome features caught in the lens of a celebrated photographer gently mocked her. She felt like an idiot, not recognising him, and it turned to anger when she thought of the way he had held out on her. Then she recalled how little time they had actually spent together and how little talking they had done. On the few occasions when they had talked most of it had been about her own problems, and he had concentrated exclusively on those.

There was certainly enough food for thought, and she felt pretty stupid to think how out of touch she had become since leaving art college. In the old days she would have been as well up as anybody on who was in the news. In fact, she realised she had seen some of Jed's earlier movies, but like most people hadn't really registered his name as producer or the name of his production company.

His odd look as he handed her his card at the beach house came back to her, and that cryptic remark he had made at the time. It must have been strange for him to discover somebody under the age of seventy who hadn't heard of him. No wonder he thought of her as a nun!

The article, she now discovered, was to celebrate the fact that he had recently won a top prize at the Venice Film Festival with his directorial début, and over the page there was a photograph of him standing against a backdrop of some watery palazzo or other. He was accompanied, she saw at once, by a ravishing dark-haired woman, titled, according to the caption underneath, and as glossy as they came. By that time Jane's head was spinning. She thought she knew him. But in reality she knew nothing at all.

Just then a shadow fell across the page, and when she saw who it was she hurriedly lowered the magazine. He didn't notice.

'Are you working this evening, Hutton?' he demanded, his eyes icing over her flushed face as if anticipating unsheathed claws.

She hesitated. Most evenings when she claimed she was working she spent the evening slumped in front of the television in the solitude of her apartment, her mind too much of a mess to permit a single coherent idea that might be adaptable to a visual treatment. Jed observed her hesitation with a satisfied smile.

'Good. In that case, we're dining out. I feel you need to meet a few people. I'm having dinner with the trustee of the Academy, and although they won't be able to help you directly, of course, it might do you good to have a proper conversation and to be seen around. You must be bored out of your skull, not meeting anyone from one day to the next.'

'I enjoy it. I'm not the gregarious type like you,' she defended, though she was already on the point of acceptance anyway.

But before she could say so Jed evidently took her agreement for granted, because he turned, saying over his shoulder, 'Eight o'clock, then. Wear something fairly formal,' and was already deep in the crowd by the time she caught up with him.

'What do you mean, formal?' she demanded. 'I haven't got anything remotely formal.'

He gave her a slow burning up-and-down look. 'Nothing?' he asked as he raised his glance to her flushed face.

Jane shook her head. That look sent wildfire scudding through her veins, but this time she wasn't going to give in to it. Besides, not only hadn't she got a formal gown, she hadn't got a title either.

'Dear Hutton, what are we going to do with you?' He gave an exaggerated sigh. 'Just a minute.' She shuddered involuntarily as the hand he put on her forearm seemed to brand her flesh with its imprint, but to her relief he went over to a group of women on the other side of the room and she saw him bend his head, then they all looked across at her.

Despite her protestations she felt herself taken in hand, conveyed from out of the office and up a steep flight of stairs into another part of the courtyard compound. Evidently Linni, to whom

Jane had just been introduced, and one or two of the others had apartments here—all part and parcel of working for Jed Mitchener, she discovered.

'He's great, isn't he?' chattered Linni as they made their way into her cosy shared apartment. 'But——' she frowned '—I haven't noticed you around before. Which sector are you working in?'

'I'm not,' explained Jane. 'At least, I'm not working for the company. I'm a painter. Jed's lending me a studio over there.' She gestured across the yard. 'He's sort of taken my career in hand.'

'He does that. He's so generous. There's always some protégée or other. He's like one of those Renaissance princes, Lorenzo the Magnificent or somebody—you know, the one who put up the money for Michelangelo and Donatello and the rest. Jed would like life to be like that all the time—art and music and everyone looking wonderful.'

She went to a large cupboard and dragged out some short evening dresses and set about finding one suitable for Jane to wear.

Jane should have had a suspicion from Linni's blonde bubbly nature that their taste in clothes would be very different. Apart from the basics of colouring and dress size they had nothing in common, as far as she could see. The other girl's taste went towards the bright and glittery, and the concept of the little black dress must have seemed like some arcane mystery to her.

Linni, for her part, seemed equally perplexed when out of the riot of multi-coloured dresses heaped on the bed Jane chose one in pink without a hint of glitter on it.

Thanking her anyway, she hurried back to her own apartment with the dress in a carrier and stripped off her day clothes to plunge straight under the shower. With half an hour to spare there wasn't even time to wash her hair. It was so long, it would take an age to dry.

Not a minute after eight she was taking the lift to ground level. The foyer was empty apart from the figure of a man, his black evening clothes contrasting vibrantly with the sweep of jazz-red carpet that led up to him. He was sitting on the edge of the desk at the far side, his head coming up as the lift doors whispered open. Jane hesitated for a moment, her image repeated endlessly in the frame of smoked mirror glass behind her.

She felt like someone else in the pink, low-cut gown. It was made of shot silk and glimmered as she moved.

Jed rose to his feet.

God, she thought with an abrupt uncoiling of the serpent in her stomach, he's the handsomest devil alive. He looked particularly stunning in his dinner jacket and a brilliant white shirt with a perfect bow-tie, and her glance slid helplessly lower to muscular thighs forcing against the expensive material of his trousers as he moved.

She watched, mesmerised, as the muscles tightened and expanded as he came towards her. He wore the image of sophisticated urban man, jaw chiselled and close-shaven, hair groomed to a brilliant sheen, immaculately turned out, while underneath she sensed the smouldering all-male animal straining at the bars. The blood sang in her ears and her mouth went dry as he towered towards her.

Dizzying at the sexual threat oozing from his body, she put up a warding hand, her breasts rising and falling visibly beneath the décolletée of the borrowed gown.

To normalise things she tried to give a carefree shrug. 'This isn't my choice,' she excused herself. 'It was the only one not smothered in rhinestones. I would never choose a dress like this in a million years.'

'I know. That's why I asked Linni to help you.' Jed had scoured every visible inch of her, noting the tiny waist made even smaller by the tightness of the boned bodice, his eyes lingering at the pearly glimpse of her breasts rising above the top, his voice a hoarse growl, harsh with desire, the sophisticated mask scarcely concealing his instant sexual response at the sight of her.

She tried to draw back, but he had already laid a hand on her arm. 'We're late,' he growled, 'let's go.'

Tonight it was a sleek black Jaguar, a predatory monster redolent with the smell of money, that floated them out into the diamond streets of the

West End. Jane sank back amid the supple leather and tried to still the wildness of her thumping heart.

Everything was on the verge of slipping from her control again. Why had Jed asked someone to lend her a gown when he knew it ran counter to her taste? The answer was clear, even in her present befuddled state.

It was because he already regarded her as his possession. She was being packaged ready for consumption. Her spirit rose up in rebellion at the thought.

Dangerously quiet on the way to their destination, he handed her out of the car at the steps of a regal-looking mansion in one of the most famous squares in London. A liveried servant stood at the top to greet them, and another one announced them to the select group within. Fever-ridden by Jed's constant proximity, Jane scarcely took in what followed, allowing herself to be passed from one conversation to another, aware that she was making an impression, but unsure whether this was because she was being seen as Jed Mitchener's latest acquisition or because she was holding her own in the conversation.

A part of her noticed that it was wonderful to be among people who cared about the things she cared about, people who loved the painters and pictures she loved, and, against the background of his home, she recognised their host, Lord Arlington, as a man of scrupulous taste and a quiet, unassuming power. Yet, she saw, he was impressed by Jed, treating him with a rather avuncular informality, as if aware that the younger man would one day inherit from him the mantle of patron of the arts.

Dinner was a splendid occasion, served amid the lustre of old silver and fine china, innumerable wines of honourable vintage passing in succession to the mellow climax of a rare port. Jed came to stand beside her as, eventually, the evening drew to a close.

'Pretty in pink,' he murmured into her ear. 'Are you glad you wore something special now? You're the most beautiful woman here.'

'It doesn't feel like me,' she told him, blushing at the compliment.

His eyes roamed over every inch of her face with a look of such blatant desire that she almost gasped. But as suddenly it was shut off and his lips curved in a cool smile. 'You should try feeling not like you more often,' he suggested. His lips taunted her, sending starbursts of sensation in all the remembered places where his secret kisses of the night had alighted. But, for her sanity, they were interrupted by Lord Arlington, and it wasn't until they were outside under the icy canopy of the October sky that she managed to warn herself to be on guard against the dangerous moments that lay ahead.

The lateness of the hour forced a little yawn as he handed her into the car, and his response was an ironic raising of the black brows. 'What, tired already? I thought artists were night owls?' he queried. 'Don't you fancy a little nightcap at a club?'

'For an artist's patron you seem to have a lot of misconceptions,' she reproved, trying to drag her glance from his intense stare. 'We have to work damned hard to get anywhere. I expect even Michelangelo didn't carouse all night when he was working on the Sistine Chapel.'

She heard him give a melodious chuckle. 'Point taken, Hutton. We'll whisk you back to your virginal bed in no time. Don't worry.'

She shivered at the thought of him whisking her back to bed, and when they reached the lift in the dimly lit foyer her slender limbs refused to obey her command. She leaned helplessly against the lift door. One hand came down on the nape of her neck, and her limbs began to shake uncontrollably. 'No, don't, Jed,' she managed to croak through dry lips. 'Let me go up alone.'

'Alone? Don't you trust me?'

She managed a slanting look from beneath her lashes. 'That's like asking if I trust a rattlesnake.'

'Or yourself,' he added succinctly with a derisory smile. 'Don't worry, my dear—I have to fly to Milan first thing in the morning.' Before she could move he planted one hot kiss on her forehead. She was trembling from head to foot and, detecting this, Jed put both hands on her shoulders and held her steady.

His body was hard, a power-house of controlled but primitive desires, and she sensed the blatant carnality of the man, his mouth sensually hovering above her own as if he debated whether to take her with or without her agreement. But they stepped away from each other at the same moment. A blaze of bright blue bored into her skull before some shutter seemed to come down over his eyes and he handed her into the lift without a word. The doors hissed shut, and her last glimpse was the lascivious curve of his lips in a smile of parting.

At least he's keeping his promise to leave me alone to work, Jane observed when, several days later, not knowing whether Jed was still in Milan or not, she had heard no word from him. In an effort to distance herself from the voluptuary he was turning her into, at least in her imagination, she even avoided the daily get-togethers after work, just in case he was back.

It was lonely, up in her virgin tower, as he called it, worse now than the weeks by herself at the beach house, for below her window she was taunted by the immense social panoply of London, its streets filled with meetings and arrivals and all the varied life of one of the great capitals of the world. It only emphasised her feelings of captivity, and she wondered how Jed's other protégées got on. In fact, a lot of questions were buzzing around at the back of her head, like who they were, how they coped with Jed and, most worrying of all, what they were doing now.

Yet it was self-imposed, this captivity of hers; she could go out at any time. It was just the very lavishness of Jed's hospitality that gave her no ready excuse to leave her studio. Every wish, it seemed, was to be granted without question, even her meals being sent up by Jed's personal household staff.

After several days of doing nothing but work, eat, sleep, she decided to have a stroll, maybe take in a gallery or two, look round the shops—anything, in fact, to get outside for a change of scene. She missed the wooden balcony round the beach house with its vistas of sunsets and wild, wild sky.

Dragging on a quilted jacket, for the days were well into autumn now, she made her way alone for the first time out of the gates of Jed's citadel, finding herself at once in the honeycomb of streets around Golden Square. Enjoying the taste of freedom all the more for the time spent indoors, she wandered around for an hour or so, glad simply to look and listen.

Eventually she turned into a small mews and with a shock realised if she continued it would bring her out near the gallery with which she had her ill-starred contract. Quickly she turned away, with the intention of retracing her steps, but then she gave a gasp, for a man on the opposite side of the street lifted his head at that moment and they both stopped dead.

'You!' he exclaimed in recognition. 'I've been trying to contact you—hey, wait!' The venom in his tone froze Jane to the spot for a moment, then, with a memory of what had happened last time she had come face to face with Ivan Clegg, she turned tail and started to run. Once started, she couldn't stop, for she could hear him shouting after her, his voice rising to a high-pitched, petulant whine when she didn't instantly obey.

Her mind numb with the memory of previous outbursts, she wove her way through the sauntering shoppers, astonished to find him still in pursuit as she turned the corner into the alley, but the great electronic safety gates were across and she heard him give a shout of triumph as he thought he had her cornered.

With a gasp she lunged for the entry-phone, but before she could even press the button he had dashed up and grasped her by the waist, flinging her back hard against the gates with a shout of triumph. All the breath was shaken out of her and she found his narrow face twisted in peevish fury inches from her own.

'Right, madam, I've got you now. And this time you're not getting away till I've had my money's worth out of you.'

His contorted features seemed to dive towards her, then rapidly, without any discernible logic, his chin jerked upwards and she had the sense of a superhuman force knocking him sideways. Then she found herself clinging to the saving shape of the man who had come to her rescue.

'All right, sweetheart?' said a voice like sandpaper, and she found herself miraculously pressed into Jed's arms, her assailant, a dazed expression on his mean features, grovelling on the ground at their feet.

Jed shook her gently from his embrace and swivelled. 'Well, my friend, are you asking for more? Because I sure as hell intend to give you more if you don't beat it!'

'I'll have you for assault,' muttered Ivan Clegg, scrambling backwards, 'and I'll get her for breach of contract, the silly little bitch.'

Jed shot Jane a quick glance, guessing the identity of her pursuer at once. He took two strides to reach him, bent down, and dragged him to his feet by the scruff of the neck as if he was of no more consequence than a mangy cat. Lifting him until they were eye to eye, he ground out, 'Listen to me, friend, and listen well. I want a copy of that contract on my desk by tomorrow morning. Whether I take legal proceedings on behalf of Miss Hutton or not will depend on you. But get this. She's releasing herself from your terms as of now. Get it?'

'Who the—who the devil are you?' stuttered Clegg, trying to struggle out of Jed's muscular grip.

'I'm Jed Mitchener, and she's mine now. Got it?'

'Look here, Mr Mitchener...' Evidently the name meant something to him. 'It's not fair. I signed her for a year. You can't just walk in and take over——'

'Can't I?' Jed abruptly dropped him. 'Just watch me.'

Ivan stumbled before recovering and backing away with a sheepish expression on his face. 'I remember your phone calls,' he said. 'We sold you a couple of her paintings in the summer, didn't we?' His face twisted. 'Thanks I get. I tried to get you more, but she's stupid and stubborn. If she'd only played her cards right and painted what I told her to paint she'd be sitting on a goldmine now. I did my best.'

'You did your best, sure, to line your own pockets,' rejoined Jed calmly. He walked purposefully towards Ivan, crowding him so he was forced back down the alley towards the street, though he didn't lay another finger on him, and Jane heard him say, 'Get me a copy of that contract, Clegg. And if I see you anywhere near Miss Hutton again, man, you've had it.'

With that he turned and stalked coolly back to where Jane was still leaning against the closed gates, fighting for breath.

'Did he hurt you?' Jed's clear blue eyes swept over her face with a fathomless expression that was neither warm nor cold.

'I'm all right now,' she managed to gasp. 'Thanks for coming up in time.'

'I saw you running like a mad thing down the middle of the road and nearly ran you over. And him. Maybe I should have at that.' His lips curved, but his eyes were still shuttered. 'I can't leave you alone for five minutes, can I?'

He pressed the buzzer on the entry-phone and a voice answered immediately.

'Let Miss Hutton inside, will you, Greta?'

'Will do, sir,' came the voice on the other side, and at once the huge gates began to swing back.

'Go inside—I've got to get the car.' He turned and prowled back down the alley. He exuded such dominance, such a feral, lord-of-the-jungle authority that Jane was reminded stingingly of his personal history, of the back-street kid fighting for survival, and now she could see it all. He had been doing this sort of thing all his life. Facing the challenge head-on like a prize-fighter. Learning to stand his ground, to force his way through the opposition, to snatch what he wanted with no quarter given. It had made him tough. It had made him violent. It had made him the champ.

As she made her way hastily up to her studio Jane gave the matter some hard thought. It wasn't that she was ungrateful for what he had just done or that she didn't respect his talent for survival in a tough world, but there was one thing he was going to have to learn, and that was that there was one victory he couldn't win. Because, as far as she was concerned, he had given the game away in the heat of his exchange with Ivan Clegg. She's mine now, he had said. Mine.

And though it gave her the shakes to hear him say it—a female response to the primitive urge to be possessed by the male—in real life there was no way she could give in. It struck at the foundations of her entire being to feel she would be no more than a possession, something to satisfy the whim of vanity, tomorrow to be discarded for a more enticing acquisition. And she saw clearly that things stood now, as always, with this one stark fact set immovably between them, and that it would never be any different.

In her own small way she too was fighting for a place in the sun. And the prize at stake was her soul.

CHAPTER SEVEN

JED'S metallic voice came over the entry-phone only minutes after she got in. He sounded surprised that she hadn't left the door open for him.

'I said I'd be right up.' He sounded peeved. 'Come on, open up.'

'I don't think——'

'Jane, open this door.' His tone was so peremptory that it brought her hand up to the chain at once. After a brief struggle with herself, she decided there could be no real harm if she was careful, and she could hardly avoid him forever. Besides, he no doubt had something important to say about Ivan Clegg and the contract.

The chain jingled as she freed it and even before it stopped swinging he was shouldering his way inside. 'That,' he grunted, with a swift scrutiny of her worried face, 'was presumably your gallery-owning friend?' His lip curled. 'I don't think I care for your choice of male companion.'

'Choice? Wait a minute.' Jane had stepped back as he exploded into the apartment, but now she rounded on him at the double-edged tone he used. 'Are you insinuating that he was some sort of romantic attachment?' she demanded.

He pretended to be amused at her outburst and treated her to an insolent up-and-down look, a slow smile sketching itself across his face and remaining there while he prowled across the room to the sofa.

'Outraged innocence,' he murmured. The remark was audible enough to bring her over to where he sprawled like a big cat, thoroughly at ease.

She glanced down at him, torn between a quickening of desire and outrage at his uncalled-for remark, then, noticing the wicked gleam in his eyes, she suddenly saw the funny side. Her and Ivan Clegg, for goodness' sake! 'OK,' she grinned. 'It's just the thought, that's all! Ugh! How could you think such a thing?' One hand brushed her forehead. The way Jed looked now, in a black leather flying jacket and black jeans, simply knocked her sideways. No one else could compare, nor ever would.

'I suppose you'd like a drink...' she paused '...as a reward for playing the part of knight errant?'

'What would you have done if I hadn't turned up?' Jed scowled after acknowledging her smile. 'I didn't like what he was doing to you.'

Jane felt the colour drain from her face as her laughter faded. It was the sort of question she would rather avoid. It brought back bad memories to hear him ask a thing like that. 'He's got a vile temper,' she admitted. She turned away.

'Jane, tell me,' he insisted.

'I'll make a cup of coffee,' she threw over her shoulder, moving towards the galley.

She heard him get up. Then suddenly he was standing behind her, so close that she could bask in the familiar lemony tang that reminded her of their first meeting. 'What?' she asked on a whisper, avoiding his glance.

His own voice was like sandpaper again. 'Has he ever hurt you?' There was an expressionless look on his face, masking his real feelings, and it lured her on to give a small nod of her head.

But she tried to smile at the same time. 'It's past now. I know it won't happen again.'

In a trice his arms were crushing around her, dragging her hard against him, his hands cupping her head against his broad chest, his fingers running repeatedly through the long tresses of her hair. 'God, if I'd known he'd ever hurt you I'd have broken his neck,' he muttered throatily. 'What did he do to you? Tell me. So help me, Jane, I'll break his neck anyway.'

'Please, Jed, it doesn't matter. It was probably my own fault for being so stupid as to get mixed up with him in the first place.'

'Nobody has the right to hurt anybody else except in self-defence,' he intoned. 'Nobody. And no man worthy of the name should ever hurt anybody weaker than himself, least of all a woman, and I don't care if that makes me sound old-fashioned.' He cradled her against him, rocking her back and forth as if to keep her safe under his protection.

For a moment she almost forgot that in a different way, a more subtle way, he was as violent in his actions as Ivan Clegg, but whereas Ivan, like most bullies, could be scared off by somebody bigger than himself, Jed was the type to go all out until the end. The way he fought, though, was by force of personality. He didn't need to use physical or verbal violence. He could get what he wanted by other means.

Carefully she disengaged herself from his arms and moved away. The slight jerk of his head showed that he had registered her more than physical withdrawal. It brought a look of puzzlement to his face, but he didn't question her, merely watching covertly as she put the coffee on to percolate, two vertical lines furrowing his brow showing the extent of his perplexity.

They went back into the sitting-room, Jane leading the way with the tray, Jed following, silent for once, the furrow on his brow betraying his doubts.

'What are you going to do when I start filming again in November?' he asked as she poured the coffee.

'Do?' She raised her head. 'What I do all the time, I suppose. Paint.'

'What if he comes around again? Or some other similar guy?'

She shrugged. 'I can usually look after myself.' She set the coffee-pot down. 'Where are you filming?' she asked, careful to keep her tone level.

'Poland.' He gave her a swift glance. 'Then back to the States. I'm only here for post-production on the last movie. It'll be finished within the next three weeks. Then some time off, and after that a header into the next script.'

'You're very busy,' she remarked.

'Right now, yes. Take it while you can get it, that's my philosophy. It won't last.' He stared moodily out of the window.

'Of course it'll last,' she said, shocked by the sudden descent of something unmistakably black over his usual aggressive optimism.

'Probably, if I wanted it to.' He gave her a storm-laden glance. 'But I'll suffer burn-out before long, then what? I've no intention of spending the rest of my life going through the motions.'

'It'll be a long time before that day comes,' she murmured, her senses reeling at this glimpse of yet another facet of this man she kept imagining she'd got neatly filed. This time he betrayed cracks in the edifice of self-confidence that was so unexpected she was taken aback. It released a sudden feeling of compassion for him.

He gave her a sombre glance. 'You're all right. You've got it made—you and all the others like you.'

For a moment Jane thought he was referring to other women, to the harem she strongly suspected existed, but he went on, 'Movies are transient, but art—that goes on forever.'

She said, 'Only great art lasts. Not many of us can hope to achieve that. We simply drive ourselves on because we have to.'

Their eyes locked in a moment of deep understanding. He really did understand what it was like, and he too provided something lasting, for it was essential for someone to fulfil the role without which no artist had ever been able to survive. 'You are needed, you know.' Her voice was soft. 'Men like you,' she added as she saw him lift his head. 'Without patrons most artists would starve in their garrets.'

Shortly after that he had to return downstairs. But as the door closed there was a new depth to the glance he gave her. Even though he didn't kiss her this time it made Jane feel shaky, but in a different way from the violence of sexual hunger he had aroused on other occasions. It was a strange dislocation, like falling in love.

She went to the window and stood there for a long time, tall and slender, long hair flowing down her back, her wide eyes thoughtful. It wasn't love, it couldn't be, because despite what had just passed between them Jed's lifestyle remained that of a barbarian, at least in his predatory attitude to possessions, and she couldn't see them ever reaching agreement on that.

'Are you working? I need to talk over this contract with you.'

Jane stifled a yawn. She was still half asleep. After Jed had left yesterday the ideas had started to flow, and it had been well past midnight by the time she'd collapsed into bed.

'Jane, are you listening?' There was the usual impatient thrust to his speech.

'Yes, I'm still here. I was just trying to see what time it is.'

'Time for a mid-morning break, I should imagine.'

She pulled a rueful face as she caught sight of the clock, relieved that he couldn't tell she was still in her bathrobe. 'Give me five minutes.'

He rang off.

Despite his abruptness there was almost an element of cordiality in this exchange—not in the words, but in his tone. It was warmer somehow, more understanding. At least, she felt it was, but maybe it was more like a change in herself.

It was new territory, his office suite, and Jane tried to remain unimpressed as she waded through yards of dove-grey carpeting to reach the white suede visitor's chair one of his assistants pulled forward for her.

A workmanlike glass bench fulfilled the function of a desk, augmented by a battalion of screens in the open-plan section powered by a team of assistants. When he came in and took the seat behind the desk, designs for what appeared to be a film set were spread out in front of him, but he pushed them to one side and opened a leather document wallet. 'This is a copy of the contract you signed.' He pushed a sheet of paper across to her.

There was her signature. Now it all seemed so long ago. She nodded.

'On the face of it there doesn't seem to be much we can do except pay him off, but I'll get my legal guys to give it a read. We'll get you out of it somehow or other,' Jed assured her.

'It didn't really register that it was binding,' she admitted. 'All I remember thinking at the time was how lucky I was to have an offer to show my work and how could I persuade Ivan to extend it for longer than a year.' She bit her lip. 'It's lucky I never got around to asking, otherwise I'd have mortgaged myself forever.' She looked up. 'When I let you persuade me to—I mean, if I'd known it would probably affect our arrangement I would never have got involved. I suppose it means you won't be able to handle my work until this runs out?'

'Does it?' His face was impassive. 'I thought you understood my terms and imagined you could play us off against each other.' He looked down. 'That's why I've been so touchy.'

Jane accepted his explanation. 'But what if I can't get out of it, what then?' she asked with a frown. 'I suppose you'll want me to go back to the beach house.' Her eyes avoided his for as long as she dared, but when he didn't answer her glance was drawn to his.

Their eyes held for a long moment before Jed gave an impatient jerk of his head. 'I don't think so. Not yet, anyway.'

A stab of misery lanced through her. No, he would want her around at least until he tired of her.

There had never been any attempts to hide that painful truth. Her thoughts flew to his other protégées, trying to imagine how they had managed to cope when his patronage came to an end.

'Anyway,' he was continuing, 'I shouldn't let Clegg worry you—I can't see a no-hoper like him getting the better of me. And I'm sure he has his price, like everyone else.' His eyes gazed bleakly at the top of her downturned head. 'You can go now, Hutton. Don't let me distract you from your work.'

Feeling dismissed and somewhat disappointed that she hadn't managed to ask him a few questions concerning her predecessors, Jane got up, but he called her back before she reached the door. 'When am I going to be able to inspect my investment?' he asked softly.

A shudder of unbidden desire shook through her at the blatant double meaning in his request, and she steeled herself to make a non-committal reply.

'I can't wait long, Hutton. I have to leave for the Continent again at the weekend.'

She mumbled something about later in the week, then that things were only at the sketch stage, before beating a hasty retreat.

So, she thought as she made her way back to her solitary tower, he was off again. An image of the dark-haired woman in the photograph floated into her mind. She hadn't doubted that Jed had paid her a visit when he had taken those few days off to fly to Milan. And now he was going back again. Before that, though, he was going to come and see her. Feeling like hell, she tried to see his departure as a lucky reprieve.

'Jane, my dear, do forgive me for disturbing you—I'm sure you're in the middle of a painting——'

'Not at all.' It was a lie, but she couldn't tell her caller that. As yet she hadn't placed his voice. It was extremely cultured.

'Jedburgh told me I could contact you if I rang his receptionist,' the voice went on.

She had only ever heard one person use the name Jedburgh. She stifled a giggle. It must be their dinner host, Lord Arlington.

'My dear,' he went on, 'would you think it terribly forward of me to invite you for a spot of lunch next week? It was so interesting to hear you talking about your work the other evening, and old men like me need the company of beautiful women to keep us on our toes.'

He was teasing, but it struck a chord, and after a little more *badinage* a meeting was arranged. Jane was quite intrigued and certainly flattered to have been noticed by Piers Arlington. He was old enough to be her father, so that made it seem all right, and when she asked herself what she meant by that she knew it was Jed's expectations she was taking into account, though why she should bother what he might think she couldn't imagine. Anyway, his threatened trip to the Continent, his euphemism for Milan, was due any day now, and his absence would make her feel more alone then ever.

It's pathetic, she told herself crossly. Why have I allowed that man to get a hold of me? We seldom meet, and when we do he's always in a hurry. We certainly don't date. And yet here I am, hideously aware of the date he's supposed to be leaving the country in order to see another woman, and worrying about what he'll say because I'm being lunched by a friend of his. She felt exasperated with herself. Even the inspection of her current work, if that was what his suggestive words had really meant, seemed to have been put on ice. Her novelty value seemed to have been exhausted already. The thought was oddly disquieting.

She was wrong, however, in all respects, for he surged back into her life that very evening. When she heard his voice over the entry-phone her heart leaped with frightened anticipation.

'Yes, I've finished for the evening,' she told him before she could change her mind. Then her hands slid to the door chain and he was coming in.

He must have been somewhere where he'd needed to impress as a serious patron of the arts, for gone was the biker's black leather and instead he wore a silver-grey suit that both enhanced and fitted in with the luxury of the apartment. He seemed tanned and fit, his black hair rather more tousled than usual, but the same white teeth, the same high chiselled cheekbones when he smiled. And the same sense of danger in the clear blue eyes.

Before Jane could recompose her racketing emotions he had shouldered his way through into the sitting-room and taken up his customary sprawled pose among the cushions on the couch. 'Your guy's a tough nut to crack. I'm not surprised you ran away,' he began. His grin, however, seemed to convey another message, sweeping automatically over her shape with a penetrating frankness that started the fire in her veins at once. She felt her breasts rise with a sudden gasp of breath. To hide the effect he was having she bolted towards the kitchen.

'Coffee?' she called through the safety of the hatch.

'Haven't you got anything stronger?' Suddenly the voice was very close. 'Or have you drunk it all?'

She turned. He was standing in the doorway, one hand resting on the door-frame in a stance that exposed the full manliness of his physique.

God, you're gorgeous, she wanted to say, but she knew it would be tantamount to sticking her head in a panther's cage. 'Go and sit down,' she said with a forced, bright smile. 'I'll bring it through. Scotch and soda or something else?' Her head twisted to look at him.

He was smiling dangerously. 'Or something else?' he husked. 'You mean I have a choice, Janey?'

'Don't call me that.' She bent her head and tried to force herself to concentrate on small domestic tasks, one at a time, one at a time. Open the fridge door, she told herself. Take out the soda.

'You prefer Hutton, do you? Nice and neutral. Aren't you artists supposed to be go-with-the-flow types, hot for experience?'

'Is that why you hire us?' The words were out before she could stop them, together with a sharpness of voice that cut right across the mood of the moment.

The bantering look left his face at once. 'Oh, it's that sort of evening, is it?' He jerked his head. 'Come and sit down. I've got to talk to you about Clegg and what we're going to do.'

The coldness with which he looked at her lingered like the aftermath of a snowstorm, and when she carried the drinks through she felt every step like walking on ice. Perching precariously on the edge of her seat about as far away from him as she could get, she avoided looking at him even when he began to tell her what had happened.

The upshot was that Ivan Clegg refused to release her until the contract ran its course and, what was more, he was legally entitled to do so.

'I'll go back,' Jane said quickly when Jed told her this. 'You're not going to get anything out of this arrangement, and I feel guilty at taking so much and being able to give nothing in return. If you like I'll hand over my next painting as a gift. He surely can't stop me from doing that. Then if by any chance it does acquire some financial value you won't lose out entirely.'

Jed regarded her silently when she finished speaking, and it was some time before she saw his lips move. He seemed to have weighed her words with precision, and now his voice was like dry ice. 'You appear to have squared things nicely with your conscience. In fact, it sounds very much as if you've been waiting for just this situation in order to give yourself a get-out.'

He paused, and she couldn't help flinching at the look her gave her.

'Well, Hutton,' he went on in the same cold, dry voice, 'I've got news for you. I think I told you Clegg didn't stand a chance against me, and actually I meant it. If he feels you're tied to the gallery, fine.'

She gasped, but her intuition showed her there was more to come.

'In fact, events suggest a quite interesting possibility.' He drew his lips back, but it was less like a smile than a licking of the lips before going for the kill. He said, 'Owning a gallery has quite an appeal for me. It'll be a toy for when I've time on my hands between movies.' He laughed softly. 'I've bought you, Hutton. Now I'll buy Clegg.'

Jane was stunned. Did he mean to buy a Bond Street gallery, just to make sure her work didn't go to anybody else? She asked him, 'Don't you realise how much these Bond Street premises cost?'

'He may have it on a lease.'

'In which case—oh, well,' she corrected, 'I suppose you'll find a way of getting round that one too.'

'Yes,' he agreed, 'I expect I will.'

CHAPTER EIGHT

JANE remembered how Carrie had repeatedly told her that life was all about power. And now she realised she had never really understood what she meant. She had thought she referred only to the question of the control it was wise to exert over one's destiny, especially in order to fulfil a talent, making her think it was something akin to self-discipline. Getting up in the morning to start the day's work. Planning a proper schedule. Preparing paintings for exhibition. Being on time for appointments—that sort of thing.

Now she saw it was a dimension she hadn't dreamed existed.

Jed's ambitions made her own look puny by comparison.

'All that just to prove a point?' she muttered after she'd taken in the fact that he was serious about buying the gallery. 'Surely not?'

'I don't know about proving a point. All I know is what I want is what I'm going to get.'

'But you can't buy everything you want,' she couldn't help saying.

He surveyed her across a limitless arctic wasteland. 'Can't I?' His voice dropped to a hush, lips clamped, a nerve at the side of his mouth flickering with the force of some terrifying emotion barely held in check.

'Other people have desires too,' she pointed out. 'What happens when they clash?'

He was very still. 'We'll see, won't we, Jane, dear? We'll just have to see who can hold out longest.'

Then she realised she hadn't imagined the double reference to his words at all. It wasn't just the gallery he was talking about. Ice crushed along her veins, bringing her breath to a standstill.

'Yes,' he growled, probing her reaction, 'you do understand me. You always have.'

Suddenly she wanted it all to be over. Ice turned to fire. The tension of not knowing when he was going to make a move, of knowing that if she put a foot wrong he would be there to swallow her up, was too much to bear. A long shuddering breath escaped her and she leaned back, neck arching, limbs turning to rag-doll bonelessness. Flame seemed to lick the very centre of her being and she wanted to cry, Take me, use me, I can't fight you, but such was her emotion that the words snagged in her throat.

She could feel the probe of Jed's blue eyes pick and skim over her entire form. He saw what she wanted, he recognised the point at which she surrendered. But he didn't come to her. He tortured her by drawing out the moment as if she were impaled on a wire like a butterfly under the magnifying lens of a collector, fluttering with life, but unable to free herself while he forced her to undergo his clinical scrutiny.

He said, 'I had a long talk with Clegg. He told me you refused to paint the sort of thing he was willing to sell.'

'Yes,' she whispered, only half aware of what she was saying. She fluttered a hand over her hair.

'What did he want?'

'Oh, paintings that were like the ones he'd already had, but different colours. Stuff I could see was destined to be interior décor and not much more,' she managed to say.

'You told him so?'

'Of course.' She couldn't keep still, but she couldn't get up and leave either. Her hands clasped and unclasped as he subjected her to his examining glance.

'What did he say when you refused?'

Both hands fluttered up to her face again and she covered her eyes. 'He wasn't very pleased,' she muttered.

'That's when he threatened to take you to court in breach of contract, is it?'

She nodded, hands still over her eyes.

'Did he get physically violent?'

Jane shook her head. 'Not quite—well, a little bit. I was—I feared he was going to get really violent. But in the end it was more what he said that—that really——' She broke off, unwilling to relive the experience of having her emotions trashed yet again. There was a slow burn in her groin that had nothing to do with the words they were exchanging now.

'Hutton, I'm asking you, what did he do?' The soulless blue eyes bored into her skull.

She shook her head from side to side. 'Oh, don't, it really doesn't matter any more. I've forgotten it.'

'Liar,' he said softly. 'Did he do the usual hatchet job, then? Told you your work was no good?'

She nodded, her fingers still fluttering over her face, winding and unwinding in the tendrils of her hair.

'And like a fool you believed him? You'll need more resilience than that if you're going to survive,' he observed.

Jane looked up, her eyes very bright. 'I am resilient. It was just the way he banged at them that got to me.'

'He what?' For a moment Jed lost his inquisitor's look, his eyes lightening a little.

'He sort of went up to my paintings—they were hanging on the wall in the gallery,' she told him. 'It was after hours, and there was nobody else around. The lights were out. It was sort of shadowy, a bit scary, especially when he started to rant and rave and kind of grab at me. I'd brought him a couple of smallish new pictures in and he told me he didn't want stuff like that. Then he smashed his fist into one of them, said it was trash. People wouldn't buy the serious stuff. It was seeing his fist smash into it, like a physical blow, like a rape.' The word caught in her throat.

'Did you retaliate?'

'Are you joking?' She lifted her head and gave him an astonished smile through her hair. 'You saw what he was like.'

'Just wondering.' His glance slid over her face with a suggestive tilt to his lips. He got up and came towards her. 'If I touch you now, is there a danger of getting claw marks down the side of my face?'

Pinned resistlessly into her chair, Jane sank further back, chin tilting, her lack of fight the sign he seemed to be looking for. Two fingers slid under her chin and fingered it as if it were silk. It seemed as if she was sinking slowly into a pool of molten honey, first the soles of her feet, then her legs, her thighs, groin, stomach, waist and hips, then her breasts with thrusting, quickly hardening nipples, then a hot tide of it right over her head.

His fingers seemed to lick inside the neck of her denim shirt even before his very real fingers did the same, and her breasts lifted in anticipation of their touch. She felt her legs open a little, taking the pressure of his knee as he bent towards her. With a gasp she offered her mouth, her lips opening to accept his tongue, heat on heat, seeking deeper as if to ransack some unreachable chamber, then he was crushing down, his whole body hard and hungry against her own in a frantic unchaining of desire.

They uttered no words in what happened next, only the hurried rasp of a belt buckle, the rending of buttons from the front of a shirt, the hiss of tearing cloth to accompany their undressing, and before Jane had properly understood what was happening to her both hands were clasping the dense muscles of his back, feeling their rhythmic expansion and contraction as he strained against her. His body was like velvet over steel, washing her in its male scent, melding with hers in a timeless rhythm as he drove her to a delirium of desire.

Almost unconscious of what she was doing, she felt him driving into her again and again, the blood pumping through her veins making her skin flush, her breasts hard and erect as he splayed his fingers over their enticing roundness.

'Do you need me?' he asked in a hoarse, emotion-charged voice. 'Do you? Tell me, Jane. Tell me the truth.'

She felt him withdraw, his shoulder muscles bulging as he raised himself up in order to scrutinise the expression on her face.

Driven to madness by his withdrawal, she raked his back with her fingers. 'Yes, yes,' she cried out, the words spilling heedlessly from between her lips. 'Please, Jed, take me, take me.' She could pretend no longer, for she was desperate with the blind hunger to possess.

He rolled her over and over, and she could feel the soft carpeting caressing her limbs, every nerve-ending sensitised to an unimaginable pitch so that everything served the eroticism of his touch, and she moaned in his arms as he parted her legs again.

'I wanted to take you slowly,' he rasped as his breath quickened, 'but I'm out of control, I can't help myself. You've driven me to this, Jane, driven me wild. I want to take you again and again and possess you completely.' He rose over her, forcing deep inside her heated womanliness, and then he came with a hoarse cry, her own cries mingling with his, peaking, slowly dying, and then it was over.

He held her tenderly, rocking her back and forth in his arms, and his voice was like milk and honey as he whispered, 'Why did you deny me for so long when you wanted me like this from the moment we met? I saw you on your balcony looking down at me and read it in your eyes. You shocked me with your beauty, and I don't know how I managed to keep my hands off you till now. But I promised myself I would hold back until you couldn't help yourself.'

His tongue licked over her nakedness and he stopped talking for a moment, but then his fingers took over where his lips left off and he said, 'All that first evening when we were sitting in the lamplight on opposite sides of the room all I could think was what I wanted to do. I wanted to undress you, but slowly, slowly, savouring the sensation as you revealed yourself inch by inch to me, until you were ready to let me love you.'

He rested his lips against her own and she felt them move as he said, 'And now you're mine, forever mine.'

* * *

'I've cancelled my Milan trip,' Jed told her, coming to stand in the bedroom doorway with his golden body unashamedly naked. Her glance lapped helplessly over him, lifting only with an effort to seek his beloved face. They had spent the night together, and she had heard him climb out of bed when it was light and talk long and urgently into the phone in the other room. She had been too replete with a night of love even to raise her head to ask what he was doing. But now she knew, and it was all right, and she gave him an indolent smile from among the pillows. This was happiness.

'I'm glad you've changed your plans,' she told him. 'I couldn't have let you go anyway.'

He raised his eyebrows. 'Couldn't?' He climbed back in beside her. 'I'll fix breakfast for us in a moment or two,' he promised in a murmur as he began to caress her smooth flanks.

It was some time before he kept his promise, but it was worth waiting for. 'How did you manage fresh croissants?' Jane demanded, feeling the butter melt in her mouth and begin to dribble down her chin.

'I've got my staff sorted out,' he told her, 'and they in turn have the French baker's down the road under their thumbs.'

'That's you all over,' she replied, snuggling against him, replete in every way. 'Head of a great chain of command. What do you do when people don't do what you want them to?' It was a joking question, because now, after the way he had made love to her, she felt safe in his arms. It seemed inconceivable that anything could part them.

'What do I do?' He glanced down at her and kissed the top of her head with his buttery lips. 'I throw them out, of course,' he chuckled, 'without a stitch on.'

'You!' She tickled his ribs. 'I hope that's not a threat!'

'Lover——' He swept her into his arms and kissed her thoroughly before pinning her arms above her head. 'You won't put me to the test, will you?'

In answer she raised her hips, and his kisses became more possessive still.

It was well into the morning before he reluctantly said he would have to go. 'I thought you had work to do as well?' He frowned. 'Slacking already?'

'Slave-driver,' Jane chided.

But he pulled the covers off her and yanked at her legs. 'Come on, lazybones. Or we'll have to make up lost time tonight. And I can think of better things to do right now.'

'You mean to *do* right now, or you can *think* of them right now?' She lay back invitingly, half teasing but in reality willing him to come back to her, for already she was wanting him again.

Jed gave that impatient jerk of the head. 'Seriously, I must go. I've got an important deal going through. As well as——' he gave her a reproving glance '—a first offer to make for your little gallery.'

'*My* gallery?' she echoed.

'I shall make it yours,' he told her. 'Only painters who fit with what you're doing will get on the books.'

'What about the ones already on?' she asked, sitting up.

'Tough,' he said, walking out before he could witness her shocked expression.

'Jed, darling...' She followed him through into the bathroom. 'I hope you didn't really mean that.'

Shower water gave his skin the sheen of brass. Jane thought of the telescope through which she had first seen him. It seemed a world away, and another more magical world had started spinning that day.

There was a smile on his handsome face as the jets of water slicked over his muscular torso. 'What's that?'

'I mean about other painters, because they don't fit with me.'

'No point in buying the piper if I don't call the tune.' He was grinning, unaware of how she felt, and she had to reach out and touch his shoulder.

'I don't want preferential treatment just because it's me,' she told him.

'It's you, darling, because you're good. But you'll have the final say in things, no one will lose out.'

As soon as he was out of the shower he was a tornado of haste, throwing on the grey suit after he'd disentangled it from her things where they still lay on the sitting-room floor, and disappearing with a promise to talk to her later in the day. 'Work now,' he shouted over his shoulder. And then he was gone.

Despite her lack of sleep the morning flowed like a dream after that. At some point Jed came up with a light lunch of bagels and cream cheese, and they ate them together in the studio among the paints and canvases, then he had to get back to meet one of his colleagues from the States. 'We'll dine him in Chelsea tonight. Got anything to wear?'

Jane looked doubtful, but when she saw a planning look come over his face she shook her head. 'I am not borrowing anything of Linni's again,' she said flatly.

'Fair enough.' He grinned. 'But I wasn't going to suggest you did. It'd be more sensible to go out and buy yourself something.'

Before she could make some remark about not having money to squander he kissed her on the forehead. 'I'll leave something with Greta in Reception,' he told her. 'See it as payment on account.'

He left her with a small frown on her face, but she thrust her niggling little doubts to one side and picked up a paintbrush.

Now it was late afternoon, and his call had interrupted her just as she was applying a new colour. 'Got anything yet?' he asked, coming straight to the point.

Her thoughts had been miles away, concentrating on her work. 'Anything what?' she asked.

'To wear tonight,' he reminded her with a hint of impatience.

'Oh, I forgot. I'll just have to wear what I have——'

'Look, sweetheart, don't disappoint me. I want to be proud of you. And he's a very special guest.'

Jane sighed. 'I'll go out now.'

Jed named one or two shops she might try in nearby Bond Street, and she wondered how it was that the names of women's dress shops managed to slip so easily off his tongue and if he knew how much she would have to pay in places like that. Then she wondered again about her predecessors. It was something they had never got around to discussing properly, even though she felt it had a bearing on what was happening now.

But then they never seemed to discuss anything. Her frown came back. She felt stampeded by the way he seemed to conduct his life. There was no time to let things build, no time to sit and share the moment. No time to talk. And now there was no time to work either. She was going to have to put down her brush and trail round the shops.

Still, she told herself, it was very sweet of him to pay her in advance—even if he was telling her what to do with her money—and it wasn't much to ask that she looked good tonight. Besides, she did want to please him, because he pleased her too.

Smiling, she went down into Reception. When she picked up the envelope he'd left for her with Greta she discovered a gold card and a bundle of notes in case she needed cash. Greta saw her open it and their eyes met. Jane's smile faded.

'How much of this am I supposed to use?' she blurted, turning crimson at the thought of how it would look to the other woman.

'The lot.' Greta arched her brows. 'He'll be offended if you don't make the most of it.'

'He will?' Obviously this had happened before. But Jed seemed to put a label on their relationship by giving her his card. Jane felt terrible. She left the building in a rush and walked along under a cloud of indecision. If she didn't buy something to wear tonight he would be offended and she would be letting him down. But if the sky was the limit, what sort of payment was he making? Was it for her paintings, as per their agreement, or was it, as it seemed, for something else?

He had said it was on account, presumably in lieu of the paintings he would acquire, but she still felt cheap and thoroughly confused. His threat to make her his prize purchase had never seemed to ring more true.

He came up while she was still standing undecided in front of the painting she'd been struggling with all day. It was big, the biggest one she had ever attempted, and there were problems with it she hadn't even got around to working out. When she heard the door she turned almost reluctantly.

'Show me, then,' he ordered, coming straight in and taking her into his arms.

She turned with a glance over her shoulder, about to detail the problems she was facing, but he was already moving briskly into the bedroom. 'This it?' he called, picking up the dress that lay on the bed.

With a frown Jane hurried after him. 'I hope it's all right. I wasn't sure what sort of place you were taking us to.'

'Put it on. Let me have a look.'

Slightly self-conscious at undressing in front of him until she told herself it was false modesty after last night, she stripped down to her bra and panties and pulled the dress over her head. It was bronze silk and cut by a genius so that it looked as if it was moulded to her shape.

'Not bad,' he said, his eyes lazing suggestively over the lines of her body.

She went up to him and put the tips of her fingers over his lips. 'Jed, I don't feel right about it.'

'Don't be silly. It looks wonderful.'

'No, I mean about taking money. Using your card.'

'What on earth are you talking about?' he demanded.

'It makes me feel——'

'Don't say a word. It gives me pleasure. I like to see my women well-dressed.'

'Your women?' she queried.

'My women companions,' he corrected. He went on, 'Married women seem to have no problems about accepting money from their husbands.'

'Some do,' Jane assured him.

'If it really bothers you, see it as a method of defraying some of my earnings against tax.'

'You mean I'm an allowable expense?'

He took her in his arms. 'How allowable are you?'

'Don't you mean amenable?'

He laid her gently on the bed. 'How quickly does this thing come off?'

'With your around, Jed Mitchener, quicker than the speed of light.'

As she spiralled down into the strange inverse heaven of his arms Jane still couldn't shake the feeling that his generosity was part of the price he thought necessary in order to purchase what he wanted, namely herself. But it was a more complex thought than she had at first realised. Now, though, she ached for the obliteration of thought, for the total loss of self, for submission to his manful grasp.

CHAPTER NINE

'DO YOU need me?' Jed had demanded, and not until Jane had demonstrated the extent of her own sexual needs had he seemed able to continue their lovemaking. It was as if he could not get enough of her reassurances that she needed him, hungered for him with a greed equal to his own, and demanded her continual demonstration that it was so.

Yet two days later he was leaving for Milan again.

She heard the news via the intercom, an impersonal go-between, and it seemed to fit with the sudden reversal of their roles. Now it was she who needed reassurance, and all the old fears began to seep back into her mind.

She remembered the photograph of him in the magazine with the good-looking contessa and the exotic Italian palazzo in the background, and reality seemed to lurch into her frame of vision with all the vicious clarity of truth. She was a whim, wasn't she? A novelty. Just one of a long line of 'protégées' bought by a bored and wealthy man to satisfy his carnal desires. He had told her everybody had their price. Hers was an apartment and a wardrobe full of clothes. She smoothed the skirt she had just put on to go out in, and felt like ripping it off and throwing it across the room.

How she hated him! Hated herself! Why had she been so blind as to fall for him? It had been obvious from the first what he was like. Yet he had given her no love promises, and it was her own fault if she felt betrayed.

When he came up to say goodbye her mind was full of self-recriminations and she didn't look at him, pretending instead to be busy shuffling through some papers as if she couldn't wait for him to be gone. Sensing her black mood at once, he remained in the doorway.

'Jane? I'm leaving now. I just came up to say goodbye.'

His choice of words seemed to resonate with a double meaning, and she shuddered. Was she supposed to go to him, all dewy-eyed, begging him to stay—oh, please don't leave me? When she didn't reply he loped towards her, big and dark and sexy, his jaw jutting at the prospect of a fight.

He came to a stop in front of her, examining her expression with a sardonic lifting of his black brows. 'A goodbye kiss?' he enquired, lips taunting, demanding a response.

She drew back.

'Come on, Jane, what's wrong?'

'Nothing.' She shook her blonde head and avoided his glance. How could he be so hateful and so desirable at the same time? she wondered, blinded by the desire to reach out to him.

'Nothing?' he repeated, disbelief in his eyes. 'So kiss me, then.'

It was a challenge. He brought his mouth close, waiting, gauging her response, forcing her to make the choice. She froze, unable to pull away yet defiantly refusing to offer her lips.

His head remained lowered, tantalisingly close above her own while he reached out, sliding both hands over her hips and pulling her pelvis possessively against his own in a spasm of need that amply betrayed his sexual hunger. He began to rock her back and forth, his lips still taunting hers but refusing to bridge that last little gap between them.

She was dizzying with the effort of resisting them.

'So you don't want to kiss me,' he murmured, 'yet there's nothing wrong.' The rocking movement was making her head swim, but she couldn't even unfreeze enough to tell him to stop. Part of her wanted it to go on forever, but the other part was damned if she was going to let him know it.

If she had been able she would have slid her arms around his neck and said she was sad he was leaving and would he please tell her if he was going to meet anyone special and if so where did that leave them, but she was terrified of hearing her fears confirmed and felt as if she was buried beneath layers of ice. She was the princess in the fairy-story, an ice-bound captive of the snow demon, displayed to all eyes in her block of ice. Her fears remained unvoiced.

Now he was raking her body with one hand while the other still held her clamped against him, and she could feel the seeking heat of his fingers crawling beneath her sweater, and already her body was responding to him like the traitor it was, breasts thrusting upwards, tips tingling in primitive desire to savour the thrill of his touch.

'Kiss now?' he demanded, his voice thickening at the sudden rise in the temperature.

But she shook her head, faint with the nearness of him, determined not to give him the satisfaction of instant capitulation. If only she could have said something, emptied her heart of its burden of suspicion, everything would have been all right. But it wouldn't be any good, she thought, for he hadn't an atom of feeling in his bones and would no doubt be clever enough to talk his way out of the situation. But he was touching her all over, making her shudder with repressed desire.

'Jane,' he whispered in his sandpaper voice, 'you know I have to go. I have business to attend to. Surely you can understand that?' When she didn't answer he added, 'And you have work to do.'

Jane lifted a hand and put it on his shoulder, a token attempt to push him away. 'Better go, then,' she said, her voice higher than normal. 'I was in the midst of something when you came in. I'm fed up with all this. You, barging in and expecting me to stop everything and let you maul me as if you have a right. I'm sick of it.'

His eyes darkened to cobalt, a shock like a cloud over a blue ocean, and his lips tightened. 'If that's how you feel I'd better take what I want quickly and leave you in peace.' He roughened his hold, forcing her body to arch helplessly within the power of his grasp.

Now she could feel the wild heat of passion coursing through his blood, pounding against her in a rhythmical tide, and both his hands dropped to drag her hips more fiercely against his own, bending her in his arms like a stringless puppet, but even now his lips avoiding her lips and his eyes glittering with the storm-driven thoughts of frustrated will.

'You can't always have everything you want,' she told him rapidly, 'not when you want, how you want. Not all the time.'

'Can't I? Let me demonstrate how wrong you can be.'

She heard her zip go and there was a pause while his blue eyes, bright with desire, assessed her response, and before she could bring herself to writhe away his hands were sliding up under her skirt and over her stocking-tops, and she gave a gasp as he sought and found her secret self. He smoothed her pliant body against his hard one, moulding her against him with broad, sure strokes that sent any token resistance flying.

In a confusion of arms, jaw, black hair and lips, those lips which never, ever quite touched her own, she found herself lifted against his throbbing chest, placed, displayed almost, on the parquet floor of the studio in a tumble of lifted skirts and unbound hair while his immaculate travel coat finished in a heap half beneath them.

She made another token effort to ward him off, although her body instantly responded, melting and yearning towards his touch, but he gave a hoarse groan of recognition, dismissing her pretended resistance with a thrust of his head against the side of her neck as he pinned her beneath him. Her skirt rode right up so that she could feel the rough texture of his suit against her naked thighs.

'Don't pretend, Jane. You know you want this even if you don't want me,' he rasped in her ear when he saw her avert her lips from his descending ones.

She heard the sound of his zip. Then her lids closed, shutting out the feverish glitter of desire that was sending turmoil into her heart and blotting out the seductive proximity of lips which he himself now withheld until she showed some sign of wanting them. But the ice still locked her in, holding back anything that could be construed as giving in. They were locked, both of them, will against will, neither one able to concede.

It felt unreal. She was fire and flame, burning and incandescent, here on the bare floor in the middle of the studio, and Jed was already drawing her on to a quivering summit, to a mindless flowering, a waterfall of vibrant sensation. Then and only then, when he began to bring her to a climax of physical ecstasy, did her eyes open, her lips part and the word of affirmation escape her. 'Yes, yes,' she panted, 'yes.'

And then their lips met at the same moment, the ice cracked, the snow demon was vanquished, and in the aftermath a rain of sobs was wrenched from somewhere deep inside her, struggle though she did to hold them back. They sent her clinging against him in a tumult of damp hair and salt tears while he caressed her, clasping her soft form against his rapidly beating heart in a spasm of concern.

'Don't cry. I have to leave or I'll miss my flight.' He tilted her face to his and inspected her face. 'Did you mean what you said just now?'

Her lids dropped, concealing her confusion. Then he brought his lips against her own, pressing them together as if exploring the subtle difference in texture one against the other.

'I should have left by now. I'll ring you when I get in. Work hard.'

He bestowed a final kiss on her, a savage imprint, all heat and sensuality, that left her in no doubt as to its meaning. It told her to be here, waiting for him, ready for him, whenever he chose to return.

As the door closed behind him her fist bunched against her burning lips, stifling a sudden upsurge of emotion.

It would always be the same until he tired of her. She was nothing but a captive. The word hammered in her skull. Jed had bought the right to come up here for her whenever he wanted to. She would always be seeing him leave like this, would always be the one to be left behind. He would ring her when he got in, yes, to check on her, confident she would be here waiting for him because, in the pattern he had laid down for her, she had no rights, no freedom, no possibility of being anywhere else.

Despite her resistance she had become his toy, and the studio was the toy-box to which he consigned her whenever he had other things to do.

She stood in front of her half-finished painting and howled like a baby. Why was she letting him do this to her? She felt used, humiliated at the thought that Jed could take her and make love to her any time he pleased. But she wanted more. She wanted a word, a sign, something to tell her he cared more deeply than lust.

Instead she had the uncertain knowledge that he could have left to be with another woman.

Taking what solace she could, she applied herself to her work with a manic concentration. But it wouldn't come right. Nothing worked. Colours slid into each other, lines crossed when they shouldn't. It was all wrong. It was like her life. Instead of becoming magical as she'd thought it would, it was nothing but a nightmare full of regrets for the day she had first set eyes on him. How wonderful he had seemed, deceptively heroic, striding down the heaped diamonds of the sandbanks towards her house.

That was where she could go now, she thought, suddenly remembering the paid-up rent, the key still nestling inside her bag.

She could find a way to escape all this, surely? There was no need to stay and suffer further. She didn't have to let Jed Mitchener turn her into a passive sex object. She could get up and leave. She could take her destiny into her own hands.

The more she thought about it, the more right it seemed, for what was the point in going on with things as they were? How could she go on when it would end anyway? To delay would only bring further humiliation, more memories to have to learn to forget.

Rapidly packing a few things in a bag, and careful to leave behind every one of the things he had bought her, Jane climbed the spiral staircase one last time to look round the studio. She had been so happy that first day; now her hopes were as dust. She should have known she was unable to live life as a man's mistress. Now the half-finished painting accused her from its place on the wall, and she turned from it with a hardening heart. It would remain behind as a symbol of a love that had been one-sided from the start. She had never reached him because there was nothing inside to reach—no soul, no feelings, no real love for anything but the power to possess.

She was on the point of letting herself out when the intercom gave a buzz. It was half in her mind to ignore it, but then she realised she would only be caught on the way down and it would be best to deal with it straight away.

'My dear,' came a familiar voice, 'my car is just approaching Wardour Street, and so that my poor fellow doesn't have a fit trying to find a parking place, would you be kind enough to meet us in the street?'

Oh, God, she thought, Piers Arlington. His dinner invitation had completely slipped her mind.

'Hello?' came the voice at her rather too long hesitation.

'Yes,' she managed to croak, 'if you can give me five minutes.'

'We'll go once round the block, then.' She heard the line go dead.

What to do? Jane paused. Why had she said she would go down? Then, 'Fool,' she accused herself aloud. It was already too late in the evening to catch a train to the coast. Once she'd finished her packing she would have realised that. So why not dine with Piers? Her flight from the seraglio life she had allowed Jed to impose on her could begin here.

Running back into her bedroom, she picked out one of the new dresses at random and pulled it on, then quickly changed her stockings and slipped on another pair of shoes. It didn't take long. By the time Piers's Daimler was nosing its way down the narrow cobbled street she was ready and waiting on the pavement, bright smile pinned in place.

He leaned forward and opened the door for her to jump in while the traffic piled up behind. It didn't seem real, she thought as they were whisked towards St James's; one minute she was on her way to the bleak waters of the east coast and the next she was heading for the bright lights of a fashionable London restaurant. Life seemed to have no logic. But Piers was his smiling, courteous self, and Jane settled back, determined to put heartache on hold.

'Where the devil were you? I rang half a dozen times and Greta told me she saw you going out before she finished for the night, but you didn't come back.'

It had been inevitable Jane would hear Jed's voice on the other end of the line after the half-dozen messages left in increasing stages of anger that evening, climaxing with the final one at two a.m. when she had stood in her stockinged feet listening to the irate tones of a man who thought there was only a machine at the other end.

He had treated her as if she were a machine, she thought, switching her on, and switching her off.

Slowly she allowed the receiver to slide back on to its rest. It was no good—she couldn't bring herself to speak to him yet, pretending things were going to be all right when they weren't.

When the phone shrilled again she ignored it and carried on with what she was doing.

It had been a pleasant enough evening—supper with Piers. He was sweet and perceptive, and had sensed something wrong between her and Jed almost at once. He hadn't probed but he suggested, casually, that sometimes work had to have priority.

Jane took his words to heart. There was a painting to finish, and when he left her at the door around midnight she had come inside, played all of Jed's messages back, then, taking off her coat, made her way up to the studio. There was one painting she wanted to complete above all others. She would paint it for love. It would stand as a monument to something beautiful that had had its day. It would be something Jed could look at when she'd gone and perhaps recall some of the moments they'd shared. And perhaps then he would understand something of the torment in her heart.

Her eyes were dry now. She was a husk. As she put the phone down she felt there was nothing left inside. In a few hours more she would be finished.

The clothes she had packed in such haste when she made the decision to leave were where she had dumped them in their bag by the door. She left them there and put some music on, trying to wipe her mind clean of everything but the brush on canvas and the luminous shade of blue with which she worked.

London spread like an upturned casket of jewels far below her windows. But she was unaware of it. She had painted throughout most of that day, working in a semi-automatic state, her attention focused obsessively on the canvas before her eyes.

Now it was night again. A radio, tuned to some all-night music station, effectively blotted up any stray thoughts and calmed her with its non-stop optimism. Past midnight, the entire building seemed to be asleep, not even the regular steps of the security guard in the yard rising as high as this. A clock ticked somewhere in a distant room, a water heater creaked. At three o'clock she made black coffee and took it back up the narrow spiral. She worked on until she could feel the cramp in her fingers and her lids began to droop.

Almost done, she thought. Perhaps a little more tomorrow? Now she was so close to completion that she was fated to go on to the end, as if only then would she be able to draw a neat line under the chapter of her life headed 'Love'.

Simply allowing her clothes to drop to the bedroom floor, she eventually slumped into bed, claimed by sleep at once.

Something warm lay across her face. It was sunlight. She blinked her eyes and turned away. But there was something else. In the brief second of wakefulness something had impinged on her consciousness. Now she couldn't sleep. Her eyes flickered open again and she half turned. Then her blood froze.

A dark shape was standing over the bed.

She struggled up on to her elbows. 'Why are you here?' she said hoarsely.

Jed went on staring down at her. His jaw wore a hint of black stubble and his expression was set in a satanic mask. He picked his way between her discarded garments and leaned right over with both hands planted in the pillows on either side of her head.

She couldn't move. Something in the intensity of his expression sent shivers up and down her spine. 'W-what are you looking at me like that for?' she stammered, trying not to let him see how frightened she felt.

His voice was changed, not like his own, but it was deceptively cool, level, almost reasonable. 'Where were you, Jane?'

'When?' she hedged, trying unsuccessfully to avoid his glance.

'When I rang?'

'I can't remember.'

One broad hand snaked out and gripped her tightly by the chin, squeezing hard so she couldn't move, forcing her head back.

'Liar,' he grated. She could feel his thumb rubbing the side of her chin, affirming his control, but he didn't release her. 'I ran you as soon as I landed in Milan—no answer. I rang at intervals throughout the night. Still no answer. I believe you picked the phone up around two or three a.m., but by that time I'd lost all sense of time.' His eyes were black, ice splinters skewering her to the spot. 'Why did you do it?' he rasped. 'Why?'

He shook her chin from side to side as if he wanted to strangle her, fingers biting into her flesh, and she whimpered, unable to answer. She was frightened by the vengeful look on his face, more frightened than she had ever been in her life, because his voice hadn't risen above the level of normal conversation, yet there was this hideous control, like something demonic waiting for release. Inside him there was a devil ready to explode into frenzied life if she made the wrong move.

The pressure of his fingers slackened enough to permit a little movement of her jaw and she felt them tremble with strain against her skin. 'Why?' he insisted.

'I don't think it's any good. This,' she whispered, her eyes beseeching him to understand.

'What isn't any good?' His lips scarcely moved.

'This relationship,' she muttered, wishing he would stop looking at her with that dark malevolence that chilled her to the soul. Her legs were shaking violently beneath the covers, but he wasn't to know that. She mustn't let him see.

'I thought I'd given you everything you wanted,' he ground out. 'What more do you want?'

Jane swallowed. 'I want to be free. I'm nothing but a prisoner here. I feel like a bird in a gilded cage.'

He didn't seem to be looking at her now but at something elsewhere, submerged beyond his reach.

With a sudden grating breath he jerked his head down and forced his mouth over hers, prising her lips apart, hot tongue licking inside her open mouth, then with another spasm of movement he wrenched himself away, straightening and backing towards the door. 'I see you've done some painting.

Did Greta tell you Ivan Clegg had accepted my first offer for the gallery?'

Stunned by the abrupt change of manner, Jane could only gape for a moment. Then she shook her head. 'No, I haven't, I haven't been down.'

'We'll have an opening,' he said. 'Press, critics, champagne—all that. But I'll want you to be able to show your new work. How long do you need?'

'I'd have to think.'

'Sure.' His face seemed white and strained. 'But it's got to be soon. Before Christmas. Can you do it?'

She nodded from the bed. The duvet was pulled right up to her chin and her hair streamed out over the lacy pillows. When Jed left without another word, she buried her face in them, shaking, a sense of dread taking her in its grasp.

If Jane had had a subliminal intuition that despite Jed's decision to go ahead and give her an exhibition all was not well, that there was something in the air both violent and vengeful, the ensuing days allowed it to take form.

Jed would prowl into her studio at all hours without knocking, treating the place exactly as he would his own. She couldn't tell him not to, for he had every right. But it unnerved her.

She would hear his steps winding their way up the spiral staircase into her chamber, then come to a halt behind her. When she turned he would be standing there, watching her, saying little, not making any attempt to touch her, just watching as she went about her work.

When, chilled by his brooding silences, she eventually gave up any attempts to make small talk, his brief but constant visits were conducted in silence.

Any thought of returning to the beach house had gone, for there was no way of transporting the large canvases back there, and Jed had said they were to be finished in time for the exhibition.

But apart from that it was obvious he had finished with her—why so abruptly and without explanation she dared not ask. Maybe it was something to do with his Italian friend. Maybe it was because she had not been present to receive his phone call that time, and he had been unable to forgive this breach of the rules. That, she decided, was enough to make him sever any contact. Breaking the house rules. His rules.

He was like a medieval despot, punishing the smallest transgression. The punishment he was meting out to her now was banishment. It was clear he had banished her from his kingdom, except for this one irrational desire he seemed to have to make her finish what she had started and give him enough work for the promised exhibition.

It was obvious he cared nothing about her as a person, as a lover. Her intuition had been quite correct. He was the marauding type, as she'd surmised, who, once the chase was over, lost all interest. The way he had made love to her that last time, lovelessly, had been to prove some point because she'd dared to refuse him her lips. If her heart was bleeding she concealed the fact and painted with a single-mindedness that verged on desperation.

Now she really was a prisoner, for it had been arranged that should she need anything from the outside world it would be sent up for her—paints, canvases, anything. This included food. It included a selection of clothes from which Jed told her to choose something for a film preview, and when she couldn't make up her mind every single garment was left in her room, until she tired of seeing the carriers and took them out and carefully hung them up until a later date when perhaps someone might come to remove them.

She accompanied Jed to the preview, dressed, she felt, like a wooden doll, all gloss and colour on the outside. Cameras clicked. Nobody expected her to say anything and all she had to do, apparently, was look beautiful and take Jed's arm when he led her down the aisle to their privileged seat at the front, the focus of all eyes.

He delivered her back to the door of her apartment, the *bonhomie* of his public self obliterated under the familiar silence. He had done his duty, he seemed to say, entertained her so she didn't get stale, so she could paint for him all the more effectively.

Jane cried herself to sleep that night. It was an endurance test. The battle of wills was over. He had won that one. Now he was getting the rest of what he wanted by the sheer force of perseverance. He was getting her body and soul and he was getting them cut up into little pieces, morsel by morsel delivered to him while she slowly bled from the heart.

Somehow she turned herself into a painting automaton. She even managed to answer the rare questions he asked about her work. Time was dwindling fast and the date had been set, the invitations sent.

'What about Poland?' she ventured to ask one day while she worked. There was silence, and she trailed a glance in Jed's direction.

He was handsome and dark and brooding, his black will emphasised by the sombreness of his clothes. Black leather made him look unimaginably desirable, primitive, as dangerous as sin. The familiar kick in her stomach told her she was not over him then, not yet. And he had not, would never, forgive her for trying to escape.

'I've put Poland on hold,' he told her. There was a heavy pause. 'I felt I needed a break.'

Jane had been surprised to find that every day, contrary to expectations, he had remained in London. 'What about the movie you were supposed to be working on next?' she asked.

'Eager to get rid of me again?' He gave a sardonic smile. 'Arlington would be quite a catch. You'd have a wife to dispose of first, though.'

Her brush froze above the paint, then she took a deep breath and dipped it in the turps and cleaned it without looking up. There was no answer to a remark like that. Perhaps Jed needed to think ill of her to justify the torture he was inflicting. Her spirits spiralled into the pit of hell. It was difficult to paint with blurred eyes, she decided. She turned and went over to the window.

'Dreaming of escape, Hutton?' his voice rasped behind her. When she turned he had risen from the stool and stepped forward. 'Do you hate this prison so much? These prison walls? Me, your gaoler?'

A tremble of fear made her draw in her breath. 'Is that what you want me to feel?' she breathed.

'Trapped? Yes. There's no way out.'

There was a silence.

He went on, 'You have a key to the beach house, but you never told me that. You've paid the rent up until early in the new year, but you never told me that either. You had a dinner date with Piers, but——' He shrugged. 'Yet even though I keep you here you still manage to elude me. Why is that, Hutton? Why do you want to escape?'

His irises were flecked with silver, cold, and a wild storm shuddered over Jane's defenceless body. She felt her face turn pale.

'You can't do this, Jed. Not forever. You can't keep me a prisoner here forever. You can't possess everything in the world you happen to want. It can't be done. Nobody can do that.'

He gave a replica of his old rakish smile, the one that made her heart turn leaps and bounds, but this time it struck her heart with dread. He wasn't really smiling, she knew that. He was hating her for some reason, hating her with all the power of that black heart.

CHAPTER TEN

JED went out without speaking, but later in the morning one of his personal assistants rang up to ask Jane—no, to tell her—that Mr Mitchener would be ready after lunch to take her to the gallery in order to discuss the hang.

A shudder passed through her at the term, at its double meaning, but she was waiting, standing ready in her street clothes in the foyer, when Jed eventually emerged from one of the offices at the far end of the corridor.

He was wearing a Stewart plaid wool shirt she had never seen before and dark corduroy trousers looking as if they'd been hand-stitched for him, and he shrugged a chunky Gortex jacket over his shoulders as he looked outside.

He turned back. 'Are you going like that?' He stabbed a critical glance at her leather shoes. Sleet was driving against the doors, and when someone opened them from the other side fingers of snow curled round the edge.

'Are we walking?' Jane lifted her head. It wasn't far, but she knew how he felt about being recognised on the street.

'I thought we might. We never have.'

No, they never had. They had never walked, arms linked, the way lovers did. There were a lot of things like that that they had never done in the short period of their affair. Now it was too late. She wanted to say all this, but all she could manage was a lifting of her chin. Maybe the bleakness of her expression conveyed something of what she thought, for he came up to her, his mouth softening—or was it imagination? she wondered as she tried not to give in to the desire to raise her fingers to it, but he didn't say anything. Touch me, she willed. He turned away.

'Greta,' he called, 'better have the car brought round.' While they waited they stood in the doorway looking out at the sleet. It kept turning back to rain as if it couldn't make up its mind, buffeting in peevish little storms across the yard.

Jed turned to her with an odd look and reached for her wrist, linking his fingers round it like a manacle. He lifted it as if to display the fact that he had got her handcuffed. Their glances meshed and she thought she read triumph in his, for wasn't he proving by the very gesture that he had done what he had said he would? But just then the car drove up to the door and he led the way outside.

The gallery had been completely relit and every sign of Ivan's ownership removed. In its stark simplicity it was exactly the setting that would show Jane's work at its best advantage. Despite her deep despair, she felt her interest quicken at the prospect of having a proper exhibition of her own. Only belatedly had she realised that she would be showing without the support of any other painters. Jed seemed to think it was best for her that way.

Everything was turning out well, it seemed. The young woman Jed had appointed to run the place, Camilla, was someone Jane recognised as having already cut quite a figure on the art scene, and she was bubbling over at the prospect of organising the private view. Jed's PR people were involved too, and all it needed was the final draft of the catalogue after the positioning of the paintings had been decided.

Jed got into a discussion at once with Camilla about which painting should go where, and Jane was astonished to discover that he had taken such notice of them. He seemed to know them as well as she did. There was little for her to do but agree with everything he said. Afterwards, as they were driven back in the car, he turned to her.

'Your first one-woman show,' he said. 'Are you frightened?'

Jane shook her head. 'They'll either make an impact or they won't. Nothing I can do about that at this stage.'

'You seemed subdued in there, was all,' he remarked, searching her face for clues.

Conscious of the driver, she could only drop her glance. 'What do you expect?' she whispered.

'You'll be free soon enough. After the exhibition you'll be able to call the shots. You won't need anybody then.'

They were already pulling up outside, and Jane felt herself bundled out into a squall of sleet. She ran, collar turned up, into the shelter of the building, but when she turned Jed was still inside the car. She saw the door close and his hand lift behind the glass, then it began to pull away. Torn by the abruptness of his leavetaking and the sense of something not quite said that should have been said, she ran out into the yard after him, but the car was disappearing slowly through the gates, and she told herself it was imagination that had made her see the blur of his backward glance and the dipping of the dark head within suggesting he had observed the way she had been left standing in the snow.

Tears scalded her eyes as she turned back. If he had seen her he hadn't given the order to halt the car. He must feel there was nothing more to be said. He was freeing her, and he was making it clear. He had done what he promised, and soon she would be on her own.

The build-up before the private view passed in a fever of activity. Now her fatalism vanished in the anxiety of wondering how her work would be received and whether Jed's faith in her was misplaced. More than anything she didn't want to let him down.

He was in and out of the studio almost every minute as if he had to check and double-check each brush mark she made, for she was still working on one last canvas. 'Have an early night,' he ordered as the big day approached. 'I don't want you to be too bushed to talk to the critics. You're going to be on show as much as your paintings this first time. It'd be a pity if you didn't do them justice.'

Jane ran a hand through her hair, feeling the blue band slip a little. He made her confused when he looked at her like this, with that intense expression as if his thoughts went too deep for words.

'It's going to be all right,' he told her. 'This is only the beginning. You'll be a star.' He seemed to move closer, but she was in such a state that she didn't know whether she was simply imagining what she longed for or not, and she stepped back anyway, just in case. If he touched her she would do something desperate and humiliating. Better this wall of ice between them. She turned away.

'You're the expert on stars,' she said flippantly over her shoulder. 'Are you going to tell me what I should wear? Groom me to the last little detail?' She swivelled to look at him. 'Decide what image I should have?'

His colour changed, whitened, normalised, all in a flash. 'Have I been so autocratic that I've taken away all your initiative?' He watched her reaction closely.

'Not quite all.' Jane lifted her chin.

They didn't meet again until shortly before it was time to leave next day. The view was scheduled to begin at six o'clock and would go on till eight or nine, depending on its success. There was even a chance it could all be over as early as seven, Jane warned herself nervously, one quick glance being enough to tell people she was useless, just as Ivan had told her.

Jed was going on ahead, but the car was sent for her and she arrived alone just before six. There was hardly anyone around. Camilla, looking chic in an expensive fitted dress with matching jacket, was talking to Jed and a man Jane didn't recognise beside a table set with drinks and canapés. Silver buckets of ice stacked with champagne stood at the ready, and a couple of Jed's domestic staff had been brought in to circulate trays of extras among the guests. If there were any, Jane thought gloomily. There were private views every week of the year, and why should anybody come out on an evening like this to see the work of an unknown?

She sidled in through the door—and stopped. It was no use hoping to remain inconspicuous in flame-yellow, but for a moment she tried. Her glance was divided equally between the paintings, now under full lighting, gleaming like precious gemstones, more alive than she had ever seen them, and Jed.

Her heart stopped at the sight of him. Her glance devoured him with a passion she was unable to contain. But it didn't matter. No one had noticed her yet.

Camilla turned and said something. Then Jed, his eyes luminous, turned towards Jane and over the vast expanse of polished floor his glance rayed out, piercing her, dislocating her mind with the power of the message in it.

She was his, he seemed to say, possessed once and forever.

Yet he was letting her go—she as good as had his word. Shaking off the feeling he had managed to project, Jane made her way nervously towards the group, wishing madly that Carrie had been able to come down from her retreat in the Scottish Highlands. If she needed allies, tonight was the night. But the first bottle of champagne was cracked open as she neared, then a party of people came through the doors behind her and suddenly the carousel began to turn.

Jed, she had to admit, played his part beautifully, ensuring that when he was required he was close at hand, and when the situation asked for her to field the ball on her own he withdrew to a diplomatic distance. But when he thought no one was looking, his eyes brooded over her all the time, stinging her with sweet venom, at once a provocation and a caress. Jane couldn't understand what this febrile current passing between them meant. They both knew it was as good as over between them.

He confirmed it emphatically partway through the evening with a choice of words that struck her like daggers, making her reel.

It was when a columnist from a big London daily began to probe her personal life. He wanted to know how long she'd known the famous Jed

Mitchener. Whether she'd visited his ranch in Nevada. Whether they had made any future plans together. And he scribbled all her non-committal answers into his notebook with a sardonic smile on his face.

'And,' he asked in conclusion, 'how much do you think your personal relationship has contributed to your current success?'

Before Jane could begin to frame an answer she was conscious of Jed at her side. 'There is no personal relationship between Miss Hutton and me. No more,' he added with his smile switched full on, 'than between any other patron and artist. Her success, which is obviously going to be considerable, is due entirely to her own very special talent.'

The critic seemed taken aback by Jed's unequivocal defence, but he made one last throw. 'So there is no question of any personal involvement between you and Miss Hutton, and,' he continued, 'your liaison with an heiress to an Italian banking fortune is still on?'

'There is no question of any personal involvement between myself and Miss Hutton. Take that as fact.' Jed's blue eyes conveyed the warning to the columnist that he had just stepped over some boundary into dangerous territory. The man snapped his notebook shut with a little bow. The incident was apparently over.

But Jane felt she had been put through a mangle. Jed had certainly pulled no punches. There's no personal relationship. No personal involvement. Take that as fact. What had she expected him to say?

Her insides felt as if turned to blood, rising up through her body in a blinding flash-flood she could do nothing to stem. Milan, she thought. She hated it. Hated it!

Something, however, some instinct of self-preservation, kept her circulating, circulating and smiling, playing the part of a rising star, and by the time the evening came to a close her cheek muscles ached with the effort of keeping her smile in place. She endured it, one minute at a time, each successive moment a small victory in self-control.

One thing, there was no doubt she had been a smash hit. Long ago Jed had said one hit could make you and one flop could finish you off. Well, now she had the hit and was sure of the truth of what he said. What she hadn't bargained on when she went after the grail was the hollowness that accompanied it when love was absent. It was an emptiness no amount of success could fill.

Everybody seemed reluctant to leave, and to her astonishment several sales had been made for the bigger pieces. Camilla took her aside and in an excited whisper gave her the names of the buyers, two of whom were well-known with noted collections.

She tried not to feel too overwhelmed. New painters were often picked up and put down by wealthy trend-setters avid for the flavour of the month, with little concern for what happened after the painters had fallen from fashion. Presumably they were expected to go back to their garrets and carry on till they dropped. Jane had had no intention of letting it happen to her, but now she wondered. If Jed saw the relationship as non-existent, maybe he would sell the gallery on as rapidly as he had acquired it and she would be thrust back among the ranks of the once-quite-famous. Frankly she didn't give a damn. All she wanted was to sink into the blackness of oblivion.

When the evening finally came to an end they were invited on, but Jed gave Jane a brief glance. 'I'm taking her home,' he said. 'She looks as if she's had enough excitement for one day. Our Hutton likes the quiet life,' he added, to forestall any hint of appearing high-handed.

'You didn't want to go anywhere?' he asked when they were delivered back to the studios.

'I didn't have much choice,' she replied. 'As usual, you make all the decisions.' Then a spark of frustrated gratitude made her stop, but she couldn't say the words, they stuck in her throat with the realisation that in some secret way he had got exactly what he wanted from her.

His eyes seemed dark in the dim night-light at the entrance to the building, but there was no mistaking the ruthless set of his mouth. 'You always make sure I know I'm doing everything wrong,' he said tightly. 'Never mind, you've had your show, you're a raving success. You won't need me any more.'

They rose to the residential floor in silence. Jane's heart and mind were in a turmoil, at a loss to understand the note of bitterness in his tone, but a block like granite lodged immovably in her chest. The prospect of never seeing him again was making her choke. She couldn't have uttered a word just then even if he'd asked her.

When they reached the top floor and the doors opened she gave a stifled excuse and barged away from him on to the landing. Her cheeks were flaming, and with head bent she felt her lips contort as a sudden spasm of grief shook her shoulders. The strain was becoming too much. Now there was only a pace to the privacy of her apartment, a pace away from oblivion.

Her shoulders gave a betraying shake once more before she could stop them, and then to her astonishment she felt a vice-like grip at the nape of her neck.

With an oath Jed jerked her back. He must have used more force than he intended, for the next minute he was saying, 'Sorry, sorry,' his voice, rasping on the saw-edge of emotion, as tense with passion as in those nights when they had driven each other to the bounds of ecstasy. His fingers grappled feverishly at the back of her neck, tilting her face to his, his mouth hot and demanding, searching out her own, finding, claiming it in a fever of possession.

Wild with the sense of loss that was tearing her apart, she kicked out at him, her huge eyes opening wider still as she saw the mask slip and the haunted face revealed beneath.

Suddenly the impassive man of the last few weeks was gone. Before her stood a man with a face white as pain, cobalt eyes like tunnels to hell as they pressed into her flesh, seeking in a spiralling desperation for something he could not find. A hoarse groan was ripped from his throat and he enveloped her deep within his embrace.

'I will do it, Jane, I promise. You have my word. I will let you go.' He pressed his fevered lips over her forehead as if he could never touch her enough. 'But for God's sake,' he went on in a voice like rough gold, 'give me this night. Give me this one night more.'

His body was vibrating with the passion of a primal need, moving over hers as if each atom searched its mirror in hers, the profound biological quest finding its counterpart in the other. Her body responded to his touch as it had always longed to do, his words only half understood, but the primitive desire that was shaking through her recognising a similar need within him that was too much to resist.

Somehow she found herself being propelled into an unfamiliar room. It was the penthouse suite, Jed's own place, where somehow he had never taken her before.

The importance of at last entering a little, however little, into his private life was like a cold draught. It reminded her of all that stood between them.

When he kicked the door shut behind him and began to guide her towards an inner room she pulled away, turning at a safe distance to outface him.

'I can't do this, Jed. My feelings are all twisted up. I can't make love to you knowing I'll never see you again. It would kill me.'

The words dropped like stones, and on hearing them he acquired a stunned look, staring at her white-faced for a long moment before speaking. 'But you want to leave me. You hate me. This hell is your doing.' His voice was hoarse.

Jane tried to move away, but it was as if her feet were riveted to the floor, and she willed him to keep his distance because she knew that if he once reached out for her, despite her words, she would fly to him, would give him anything he desired. 'How can you say all that, knowing you have someone waiting for you in——?' She couldn't bring herself to say the name.

'Someone else?' His face was a perfect image of puzzlement. 'There is no one else. Never will be. Don't you understand that yet?'

'I thought there was a woman in Italy,' she whispered, her throat dry at the prospect of witnessing guilt on his face.

But he gave that familiar impatient thrust of his jaw. 'You're referring to that tosh the columnist was spouting tonight? You surely didn't fall for any of that, did you? They're always trying to marry me off to somebody.'

'I saw the photograph in that magazine,' she said simply.

'I'm photographed all the time with women. It's part of the job. Milan?' he said suddenly. 'You thought I went to Milan to see someone else?' His expression terrified her. Rage of a degree she had never witnessed before suffused his face, then as swiftly vanished. 'You imagine I could get up from making love with you the way we made love——' he shook his head like a boxer after a punishing body blow '—and,' he forced himself on, 'and go to someone else?' He shook his head again. 'You can't believe that.'

With a rush of some new emotion Jane moved a pace towards him. 'What about my predecessors?' she breathed, frightened to put her doubts into words. 'What happens to them when you tire of them?' When his head lifted in puzzlement she tried to explain. 'The other artists,' she said.

Jed gave a bewildered shake of the head. 'There's a trust that deals with all that,' he told her slowly. 'There are scholarships and endowments.' Suddenly his brow cleared. 'You think I'm playing with you, don't you?' He gave a harsh laugh. 'Nothing could be further from the truth. I've never invited anyone to work and live here before. You're the first. And last,' he added. 'Believe me?'

Now she could witness the expression on his face it was a picture of the truth, and she couldn't doubt the evidence of her own eyes.

He held her glance. 'I've done everything wrong. I've tried to pin you down when I knew I should let you be free. Now it looks as if by keeping back and trying to stay out of your way, because I knew you needed to be alone to work, I've been wrong again. I bought you things so as to make life easy so you could keep your mind on what's important. But you saw it as something else. Whatever I did I somehow got it wrong.'

He punched one fist into the other. 'It was the wrong thing to do to tell you I wanted to possess you. You misunderstood. I only wanted what was best for you. I still do. But it doesn't mean you have to feel like a prisoner. All I wanted was to make you the centre of my life. I'll do whatever I can to make you happy—even leave you, if that's what you want.'

She moved another pace towards him. There was pure gold radiating from him and she longed to bask in it. 'Jed...' She could scarcely put into words the hammering of her thoughts. 'I've never wanted you to leave me. Never that. You've never been in the way. I've wanted more of you, not less. I only felt trapped here because you could come and go as you pleased.' She felt the cold sweep over her in a passion of remembrance and went on, 'I thought you were going to someone else, and it made me feel so horribly sad. And I felt it must mean you'd been playing with me—picking me up, putting me down.'

Happiness was suddenly radiating from her like a rainbow-coloured halo. There was no one else in his life, no discarded artists, no Italian contessa, no one. And he wanted her. He said he wanted her at the centre of his life.

She held out her hands. 'I could spend the rest of my days here as any sort of captive so long as I knew you were going to come to me at the end of the day and take me in your arms and love me.'

'I won't tie you down.' His expression was serious. 'But I do want to marry you. You'll be as free as you want. You won't object to becoming Mrs Mitchener?' he asked tenderly.

'Object?' she smiled. 'On the contrary!'

Stretching sensually against him, she found the words she should have known from the start were the ones he had to hear, and she told him, 'I do need you, Jed. As a patron, yes, but more importantly as a lover, as the man I adore. I want to be beside you, with you, forever. You'll never doubt it, will you, darling?'

Then the way he took her powerfully into his arms convinced her he understood, and then it was mouths, lips, tongues, his hard body curving her supple one against it, and there were kisses in a total assent of love.

Later they planned a prospect of loving and living that left nothing out. They vowed to make up for all the things they'd missed doing together. 'We'll walk together, talk together, we'll do all those simple things we never had time for before,' Jed told her.

There was the ranch in Nevada, he explained, a movie to be made, holidays in the sun and Venice and Cannes and long, lazy Sundays when they would stay home and do nothing.

Jane stopped his mouth with her fingertips. 'Yes to all that, so long as I have time to paint. Will you promise to help me as you already have, and to stay beside me?'

'Always,' he vowed. 'And I may as well tell you I have plans for a script. Things are going so well I can leave the hustling for production money to somebody else and focus on the side of the movies I like best. We'll find a retreat somewhere wonderful where we can work side by side, a studio for you and a study for me. Just tell me again you'll always want me close.'

Remembering the child inside the man whose passion was to possess the beauty denied him long ago, Jane found it was easy to say the words she had once locked away. 'I need you, darling. I'll want and need your love forever without end.'

He smiled as he drew her down beside him, and soon there were no more words, for no words were needed.

Zodiac Scramble—Word Competition

How would you like a years supply of Mills & Boon novels <u>ABSOLUTELY FREE</u>?

Well, you can win them! All you have to do is to unscramble the Zodiac signs listed below plus complete name and address details overleaf and send them to us by 31st March 1993.
The first five correct entries selected after this date will each receive a years supply of Mills & Boon novels FREE (10 novels each month). The novels are valued at over $490.00.
What could be easier? Post your entry TODAY!

SCEPSI ....

RCNACE ....

OPIRCOS ....

QUUSARIA ....

RINROCAPC ....

ISERA ....

MIGNEI ....

UURSAT ....

BRAIL ....

STARITSUAIG ....

EOL ....

GVIRO ....

Please turn over for entry details

★ HOW TO ENTER ★

Just unscramble all the Zodiac words listed overleaf then complete your NAME and ADDRESS details below and pop entry into envelope and post before **31st March, 1993** to;

ZODIAC SCRAMBLE-WORD COMPETITION
***3 GIBBES STREET**
CHATSWOOD 2067

Name (Mrs, Miss, Ms) ______________________________

PLEASE PRINT

Address ______________________________

____

______________________ *P'Code* ______________

DAY TIME
Telephone No (   )______________________________

ZSW193

*New Zealand Address: Private Bag 92122, Auckland 1020

PLEASE TICK THE BOX IF YOU ARE A READER SERVICE SUBSCRIBER ☐

Competition is open to residents of Australia and New Zealand only. You may be sent promotional mailings as a result of this entry.

ONLY ONE ENTRY PER HOUSEHOLD PLEASE

★ ★